BADLANDS JUSTICE

BADLANDS JUSTICE

Dan Cushman

CHIVERS
THORNDIKE

This Large Print book is published by BBC Audiobooks Ltd, Bath, England and by Thorndike Press®, Waterville, Maine, USA.

Published in 2005 in the U.K. by arrangement with Golden West Literary Agency.

Published in 2005 in the U.S. by arrangement with Golden West Literary Agency.

U.K. Hardcover ISBN 1–4056–3447–2 (Chivers Large Print)
U.K. Softcover ISBN 1–4056–3448–0 (Camden Large Print)
U.S. Softcover ISBN 0–7862–7894–3 (British Favorites)

The text of this Large Print edition is unabridged.
Other aspects of the book may vary from the original edition.

Set in 16 pt. New Times Roman.

Printed in Great Britain on acid-free paper.

British Library Cataloguing in Publication Data available

Library of Congress Cataloging-in-Publication Data

Cushman, Dan.
    Badlands justice / by Dan Cushman.
        p.   cm.
    "Thorndike Press large print British favorites."—T.p. verso.
    ISBN 0–7862–7894–3 (lg. print : sc : alk. paper)
    1. Large type books. I. Title.
PS3553.U738B33 2005
813'.54—dc22   2005013468

For MAMA

CHAPTER ONE

Holly Wolverton reined in his bay bronc as they turned into Box Elder's main street and said to his brother: 'Well, Joe, they're all lit up for us. Couldn't do better for Grover Cleveland.'

Holly was good-looking, especially when a grin softened the slight hardness around his mouth. He grinned now at Joe, took off his Stetson, and used his fingers to fork back his yellow hair. He was only twenty-three, but he'd been around and that made him seem older. It made him seem much older to Joe, who was still sixteen.

Joe had stopped a trifle behind. Without making much show of it, he readjusted his own hat, putting it on the back of his head, imitating Holly. He rocked over in the saddle, too, with one leg straight and the other bent; and when he looked down the street, with its saloon glare of kerosene lights, it was with his back and shoulders slanted forward and one hand on his thigh, all copied after Holly.

There was a brown-paper cigarette in Holly's lips that had been out for the last half-mile, and he lighted it now, the match making his face look lean and coppery, bringing out the little bird-track wrinkles that sun glare had already printed at the corners of his eyes.

1

He dragged and talked smoke from his mouth. 'Well, I suppose I might as well go down and let North take his whack at me.'

'At *you!*' Joe stiffened and tried to look like a man, though at that moment he didn't feel like one. He'd always been scared of North. He could feel it inside even at mention of his name. He'd seen North kill a man one time, but he tried to keep from thinking about it. 'You ain't going down there *alone.*'

'You know the rule. One representative for each outfit. That's all they vote at all these Association meetings. You drift around and look at the bright lights.'

'I'm going along,' Joe said doggedly. 'I'm not scared of North.'

'Oh, all right.' Holly nudged his bronc into motion and rode for a while before saying: 'Of course, you're not scared of North. And even if you were, it wouldn't be any disgrace. I been scared of men. Never forget the time down in Wyoming I had to tangle with a woolly wolf by the name of Black George—'

'Black George *Watson?*' Joe said with his eyes getting big.

'Yes. He's the one. I was holed up with some of the boys over at Jackson Lake, and this Black George rode over and got to telling around that I'd put the law on him and got him chased away from the Big Horn. First time he got full of trade likker, he promised to kill me. I wanted to hit for the high country, Joe, but I

2

didn't. I told myself if I ran from him once, I'd be scared of turning corners for the rest of my life. So I did the other thing. I tied down my gun and went looking for *him*. Sometimes a man will do those things if he gets scared enough. I guess he just gets so damned scared he'd rather be dead.'

'You *killed Black George*?'

'No, and he didn't kill me. I walked in to the Skynoo Kid's shanty—they always played cards there; it was sort of a saloon—and said, 'I heard you were looking for me, George.' And he said, 'Sure, Holly; I want to buy you a drink,' and that's all there was to it. You see, the other fellow's human like you. Two hundred fifty grains of lead hit a man and it kills him no matter what kind of reputation he's got. Take North, now. He might be scared of you if the cards fell right.' He rode close enough to nudge his kid brother with an elbow. 'That's what we'll pretend when we walk in on that Association meeting. We'll pretend they're all scared of *us*.'

Joe had been taut since sighting the lights of Box Elder. Despite the chill of Montana night, sweat had soaked the band of his hat so that it felt thick and slippery on his forehead, but his brother's easy voice made him feel better.

The street was wide and still a trifle muddy from the May rains. It was Wednesday and as a rule things would be slow, but the Association's annual meeting had brought

3

many men in. Saloon and honky-tonk owners were making a bid for business, with all their lights on. Music drifted down from the hall above the St. Louis Café, and someone was playing the piano at Shorty's. Along the hitch racks were broncs wearing the brands of outfits from the Musselshell to Gravelly Butte, half the way to the Dakota line.

They rode two-thirds of the length of the street and turned in, beneath the heavy shadow of cottonwoods, to the long, ramshackle Stockman's Hotel. The big second-story room was lighted, and shadows of men were visible against the mosquito bar. The hitch racks all along the street had been full, yet here, at the center of things, there were several spaces open.

Holly said: 'Don't be bashful, Joe. Just tie up any place. We're important folks tonight. We're number one on their kill list.' And he laughed, turning it off as more of a joke than it actually was.

They dismounted, stiff from riding, their levis sticking to the insides of their legs. They took their spurs off, got their clothes straightened, shirttails in, and climbed to the high front porch. Eight or nine elderly men were sitting in round-backed chairs along the front of the building. One of them, a toothless, long-haired old man called Soldier Jim, cackled and said, 'There's the Wolvertons, and it's their night to howl.'

4

It was an old joke to a Wolverton, but Holly laughed as if he'd never heard it before. 'We're a couple of rangy old he-wolves from Cactus Crick and we already lost toes in the trap.'

Followed by Soldier Jim's high-pitched giggle, they started for the door, but as Holly turned he hesitated. Joe followed the direction of his gaze.

A team and buggy stood in the shadow of cottonwoods a short distance off, and a girl, discernible because of her white dress, was sitting alone in the front seat. The girl was Ellen Eaton.

Joe had heard talk about Ellen and Holly. He'd heard that Holly had been riding over to the Goosebill to visit her when her father, Major Miles Eaton, wasn't around. But the Major had caught up with him and promised to kill him if he tried to see her again. He'd never believed it until now, but something about the brief, almost haggard expression on his brother's face told him it was true.

Holly noticed Joe watching him and jerked his eyes away. 'Well, should we go up?'

'Sure.' The men were watching them, and it seemed to Joe almost as if they could look through him and see how scared he was, so he slid his hat back like Holly's and gave his heavy-weighted gun belt a hitch. He even put a grin on his face as they went inside.

Holly said, 'Need a drink?'

He'd never offered to buy Joe a drink

5

before. It was like a public announcement that he was a man.

'Afterward,' Joe said.

The dinky lobby was overcrowded with leather chairs. Some white-pine stairs led up at the left, and there was an archway leading to a bar at the right. A heavy, square-faced man of forty had been standing just inside the arch, sharpening a match into a toothpick. He snapped the knife shut when he saw them and started forward, with light making a brief gleam across his deputy's shield. This was Wasey Slager, the undersheriff, and accidental as the meeting looked, Joe knew he'd been waiting around to talk to them.

'Hello, Holly,' Slager said, and nodded to Joe, knowing he was the kid brother without knowing his name. 'Going up?'

'Yes. How late are we?'

'Oh, you know how those things are. They been stringing in all night.' Then he came to the point. 'Take it cool. If you get into any trouble, don't expect any help from me.'

Holly answered him in a tone so soft it sounded deadly, 'You're one man I'll never expect any help from, Slag.'

Slager straightened and his eyes narrowed. 'What do you mean?' Then he went on without giving Holly time to answer: 'You mean I'm run by the Association? I wouldn't advise you to go around saying it.'

'No, I wouldn't say that. After all, *I'm* a

member of the Box Elder Roundup Association.' He used the whole title, and it gave the words bitterness. 'Did you give your bit of advice to North, too?'

'All I want to do is keep you out of trouble.'

'Thanks. But you forgot to answer my question.'

'Yes, I had a talk with North.'

'Then neither of us got anything to worry about. Tonight, in that crowd, I'll be peaceful as a jackrabbit at a rattle-snake's convention.'

On their way upstairs Joe asked, 'You think he said anything to North?'

'Sure, he talked with North. I imagine they talked about the price of beef.' When Joe called Slager a bad name, Holly went on: 'No, don't blame him. That's how the law is. It gets elected by the strongest side, and that's the side it protects. I found out about *the law* a long time ago. I found out about it down in Wyoming.'

The Stockman's Hotel had been built by the Yellowstone Stage Company to provide halfway accommodations for travelers who wished to take the shortcut from Miles City to the Milk River country rather than the big loop by way of Fort Benton. They had devoted half of the second floor to a sample room, though no drummer ever had enough in his trunk to need it, so it was used occasionally as a theater or, as tonight, a meeting place.

From outside the door they could hear

chair-squeaking movements of seated men, the drone of somebody talking.

Holly said, 'Which you prefer, hanging or shooting?' And with that he opened the door and led the way in.

The meeting had been in progress for a considerable time, judging by the layer of smoke that hung under the kerosene lamps. Twenty or twenty-two men sat around the walls, most of them tilted on the hind legs of their chairs. Joe's eyes instantly traveled to the front of the room, where Creighton North was seated.

North was a rugged, rangy man, about thirty-five years old. He sat leaning forward with one elbow on the wooden arm of his chair, chin cupped in his hand. He looked at Holly and Joe and then away, as though he had no special interest in them.

Tom Nemus of the TN was talking, and he continued until his sentence was finished. He waited, scratching the back of his thick neck while Holly and Joe crossed to a couple of empty chairs. Joe noticed how loud their boots sounded. It was a relief when Guff McGuffy, a whiskered, roughly dressed man leaned over, spat in a cuspidor, and said, 'Damn it, boys, we about decided you got sidetracked down at Dutch Molly's.' He followed with a rough burst of laughter, and most of the others joined in.

Holly jerked his head at Joe and said, 'Had

to blindfold him to get him past. He's hell among the yearlin's.'

'He ain't the only one that's hell among the yearlin's, by what I hear.'

This didn't get quite so much of a laugh. Everyone there had heard the gossip about Holly and Ellen Eaton. Besides, her father, the Major, was seated at the front of the room, chairman of the meeting. Guff, who disliked him, sometimes took the opportunity of blurting out barbed remarks that sounded as if they came by accident from his rough mouth.

Nobody looked at Eaton, except Joe, who did it in spite of himself. Eaton had listened to the words without the tremble of an eyelash. He was a thin man in his late fifties, quite handsome with his silky white mustache and goatee. There was an unlighted panatela cigar between his fore and midfingers. He sat with his spine stiff as the barrel of a Winchester, not because of Guff's words but because of his army training. When the newcomers were settled in their chairs, he nodded to Tom Nenus, who went on with what he had been saying, something about the hundred-odd strays from across the river that had wintered at Pipestone Coulee. While he was talking, Joe had time to steady himself and look around the room.

He knew who practically all of the men were. Many of them had stopped at the Winged W, the Wolverton home ranch, in the

9

days when his father was alive, before he lost his life and most of his stock in the tough winter of 1887. There was Nenus, who was talking; McGuffy and his half-breed son Pete, Barry Simmons, Tip Carslyle, Jim Sims, and old Bill Bousard, who was invariably called, and even signed his checks, 'Billy Buzzard.' But while Joe looked at them, his attention was never quite diverted from Creighton North.

North did not look like the others. He had not started out as a cowboy, nor as a cavalryman like Eaton. He had been a dirt-moving contractor with a gang of Irish immigrants when the N.P. railroad went through, and later he was a freight boss with the Musselshell line when it had an Army contract. After that he had got into the cattle business on shares with the old Square and Compass outfit, and when it went under during the tough winter of 1887 he had become general manager for the Great Western Land and Cattle, better known as the Snaky G because of its brand.

It had been five years ago, when North was still with Square and Compass, that Joe had seen him kill the man. It had been during the beef roundup. They had brought twelve thousand or fifteen thousand head along the flats of Squawhammer Creek, stopping there to cut out the Block N and Drumheller stock that had strayed through the badlands from across the Missouri River. About an hour after the work started, Jerry McBride had ridden in and started to claim steers.

McBride and his brothers had been known as maverickers. They had had a little spread near the mouth of Milk River, but it was only a blind; their real center of operations had been in one of those lost valleys down in the badlands. McBride had claimed about twenty head when North rode up and called his hand. The fight came with blazing suddenness. As North swung down from his horse, McBride had started to draw, but North, big and slow as he looked, had beaten him.

Joe had listened to much gunfight talk, but this was the only man he had ever seen killed. Even now he could remember the scene with minute exactness: big Creighton North, spread-legged, jerking his Colt upward, ramming it forward, firing with a coupled squeeze of thumb and forefinger, and McBride knocked halfway around by the force of the forty-five slug, staring, with death in his shocked, off-focus eyes.

Nenus finished and sat down. A motion was carried. Major Eaton made a notation in his book, then looked over at Holly and said, 'Good evening.' He was perfectly polite. 'We were in hopes you would come. There's a little something we want to straighten out.' He nodded to North. 'All right, Cray, let's have it over again.'

North rubbed his hands back and forth a few times across the tight-stretched thighs of his California pants. He had a furious temper and he hated the Wolvertons, but with Eaton and the others there he tried not to show it.

He started talking, addressing his words to Holly: 'First of all, there's some talk going around that I said you were a rustler. That's a lie. I wouldn't call any man a rustler unless I knew he was, and if I knew he was I wouldn't talk about it. I'd do something about it.'

Holly said, 'What would you do?'

'I only know one medicine for a rustler. A stiff rope and a short drop.'

'You mean you'd do your hanging without the Association?'

Fury gave North's face a hollow look and made the muscles stand out in his neck, but he controlled himself and said, 'I didn't say that.'

Eaton said, 'Let's leave the rustlers to another time.'

'Sure,' Holly said softly. 'Let's leave that stuff for the big seven to decide on.'

North shouted, 'What d' you mean by that?'

'I mean a thing like that is too important for all us little fellows to vote on. Just like splitting up the range was too important.'

North lunged to his feet. 'You say what you mean!'

Eaton's voice cut between them. 'We'll have no brawl here!'

Holly said: 'Us Wolvertons aren't giving up

12

the Squawhammer range to that back-east outfit that you run, North. My daddy shot the buffalo off that grass. We had cows on it while you were still jockeying a horse scraper on that N.P. construction crew.' His eyes roved the room and came to rest on McGuffy. 'How'd you vote on chopping up the Wolverton range, Guff?'

McGuffy spit more tobacco juice and said: 'Hell, you talk about your relations shooting buffalo off. My old lady's folks was shootin' the Blackfeet off there for the last five hundred years.'

'Maybe you'll have a hard winter next time and some plush-office outfit from Chicago will vote you out of the best of your range. Sometimes it works both ways.'

Guff grumbled: 'I ain't the whole shebang. I only got one vote.'

Holly's eyes roved on and came to rest on Tom Nenus. 'How'd you vote?'

Eaton cut in to say, 'If you wanted to hear the vote, you should have attended our meeting.'

'I wasn't asked.'

'You received a fair cut of the grass, more than your stock will be able to graze in the foreseeable future. Some of you old-time outfits drove two-dollar longhorns up from Texas and scattered them across the range all the way from Missouri to the Yellowstone, and when you were through there wasn't winter range for a jackrabbit. That's why the blizzard wiped you out. When we met here and divided the range, I didn't know of anybody who was satisfied. But that was all settled last summer. We have some other things to take up now.'

It sounded good the way Eaton told it. It sounded good when it was printed in the Box Elder *Prairie News,* too: 'At a meeting last night attended by stockmen representing better than 80 per cent of the total holdings between Musselshell and Gravelly Range, it was decided . . .'

Holly said, 'All right, Major, why was it you wanted me here *this* year?'

Eaton, with an icy steadiness, lighted his panatela cigar. Joe, watching him, wondered if it were true that he had threatened to kill Holly for visiting his daughter. It was hard to believe, he remained so impersonal, his fingers applying the match so steadily that they could have held thread to a needle. He finished, laid the match down carefully, with its blackened head over the table edge, and spoke.

'Mr. North was informing us that you had some sort of agreement with Lee Stickley, over at Drumheller's.'

'I'm running a few of those D bar H steers.'

North cut in and asked, 'How many?'

Holly thought the question over. 'I don't think that's any of your business.'

North shouted: 'By God, it *is* my business!

It's my business and the business of every man here. We all know what Stickley is, and we know what the Drumheller outfit is. They hogged half the range north of the Missouri, and now they'd like to move across. But they ain't getting a foothold through you or anybody else.'

Holly, smiling a trifle, sat with one leg crossed over the other, jiggling his toe, looking down at the scuffed boot toe. Then Joe noticed the rapid throb of an artery in his brother's throat and remembered Holly's words about a man being so damned scared he'd rather be dead.

Holly looked around and said, 'I bet you boys voted on it already.'

North said, 'Yes, we voted on it.'

'Unanimous?'

Chad Newhall, a bleached-out rancher who raised almost as many kids as cattle, said, 'It wasn't unanimous.'

Eaton said, 'How many Drumheller steers have you brought over?'

'About two hundred.'

'Where are they? North says they're grazing his Squawhammer grass.'

'They're on the Squawhammer.'

'Well, get them off. Get them on your side of the ridge. This question hasn't come up before, so I think we can be lenient. Get them on your own grass and don't bring any more across the river. The D bar H isn't getting a toehold on this side.'

Holly looked over at Joe, and when they took up the next question he grinned and whispered from the side of his mouth: 'See how it's done among gentlemen? It's the same old business, only here they do it so smooth you don't even know it's happened.'

CHAPTER TWO

Joe passed a hand across his forehead and looked at the sweat on it.

'Want to get out?' Holly asked.

Joe was ready to say No, but when he saw that Holly intended to go with him he said, 'All right,' and stood up.

When they were in the hall, with the door closed, Joe asked: 'What about those Drumheller steers. I never heard—'

'Oh, those. I never said much about 'em on account of Ma. You know how she is about Stickley.'

Joe knew. Ma had often said that Stickley would have swung from a cottonwood long ago if he hadn't been general manager for Drumheller. 'Yeah,' he said, 'and I know how Pa felt toward him, too.'

There was an edge to Holly's voice. 'I had to get stock on the range. Maybe you could think of a better way. But Stickley's not so bad.

16

Don't want to believe everything you hear. Far as that goes, look what they say about me, and here I'm practically a sky pilot.'

'I didn't say anything against him.'

As they went downstairs, Holly told how he'd met Stickley at Musselshell Landing and agreed to run some bone-bag D bar H steers and split half and half on the average weight over six hundred, Chicago price. The Drumheller riders had driven them over the Missouri, and he'd brought them straight up Squawhammer Creek, through the badlands.

Joe said, 'And you left 'em on North's grass?' It scared him a little to think that Holly would do such a thing.

'Always some D bar H stuff drifting across, coming up from the badlands here and there on the Squawhammer. I hoped North would think they were strays, but he found out. He's good at finding things out.'

They walked through the lobby, with Wasey Slager watching through the barroom archway. Outside, it felt cool and good. A breeze was rustling the stiff leaves of the cottonwoods.

Joe said, 'You aim to leave the steers there?'

'If I left those longhorns on the Squawhammer, North would chase them so far into the breaks nothing but a band of hungry Injuns would ever find them again. No, I'll have to start drifting them home.'

Joe noticed that Holly had stopped and was looking beyond the porch where Ellen Eaton had driven up with the buggy. She was gone now, but Alf Koenig, a heavy, flat-faced man of fifty, foreman of her father's Goosebill ranch, was sitting in one of the chairs, watching them.

Joe spoke from the side of his mouth, 'There's Koenig.'

Holly gave him a half-smiling glance and said, 'Now, why should I care about Alf Koenig?'

'I don't know.'

'Listen, if I want to see Ellen I'll see her, and Alf Koenig be damned. You don't believe that story about old Miles driving me off the Goosebill, do you?'

'I never heard anything about it!'

'The hell you didn't!' They walked across the yard, under cottonwoods, to the gravel path where the lighted saloon fronts all came in view. There Holly stopped. 'You drift down and hit the high spots. Meet you back here at the hotel. And try to keep sober!' he called over his shoulder.

Joe felt cast adrift as he walked down the plank sidewalks in his old, chokebore boots. He could hear pianos and music boxes whanging away. The high screech of a fiddle came from above the St. Louis. A woman giggled over and over, with a note of hysteria. It was all strange. It made him feel unsure of himself. He had a good notion to have some drinks and show Holly a thing or two.

18

Three men came laughing and wrestling through a door and almost rammed him off the sidewalk. One of them said, 'Why, there's Little Joe the Wrangler!'

The boys had joshed him that way to get his temper up when he was horse wrangler on the roundup, but being called 'little' didn't bother him tonight. It was too good to hear a familiar voice. The man was Dude Gallagher, who had deserted from the Northwest Mounted Police and come down to punch cows for the TN two years ago.

A tall gray man with a drooping mustache had followed to the door and said, 'You say the Wrangler's out there?'

He recognized Two-Bit Johnson, once a buffalo hunter and later a camp cook for half the outfits on Box Elder range. Tonight, he was thoroughly drunk.

He limber-legged it outside, got one arm around Joe's shoulders and said: 'Why, damn it, look how you grew! More like your old daddy every day.' He was ready to weep. 'Just so you end up being the *man* your old daddy was! We went through hell and squaw cookin' together, him and I. Now *there's* a man that wouldn't let any Chicago meat-packing outfit run him off the grass.'

Joe tried to pull away, saying, 'Holly and I ain't letting the Great Western chase us off the grass!'

'Glad to hear it. Say, you come on in and I'll

19

buy a drink for old time's sake.'

They went inside the Elkhorn, always the most popular saloon in Box Elder, and got to the bar.

'I ain't got any money,' Two-Bit confessed after digging his pockets. 'Now ain't that hell? Me ask old Clay Wolverton's boy in for a drink and here I am broke.'

Joe tossed out a silver dollar. He poured a drink and downed it. He had tasted whisky before, but not in that quantity, and it took his breath away. Two-Bit was talking:

'. . . that's what they been saying. Ned Garfield told it to Brewer, and Brewer got drunk and told me.'

Mention of Garfield made Joe pay attention. Ned Garfield had come up from Wyoming to ramrod the Snaky G for North. He was a bad one who would have had notches on his gun if he had been the kind who carved them.

'What about Ned Garfield?'

'Why, I was just telling you.' Two-Bit looked at his glass. 'Say, *you* buy *me* a drink now.' Joe paid and watched Two-Bit pour it. 'Ned Garfield said that North was buying the Winged W from your ma. That's what he said. I hope it ain't true. Damn it, Joe, this won't seem like the same country without that old sidewise W showing up on every maverick two miles from its ma.'

'We'll see Creighton North in hell before he

takes over the W!'

Two-Bit giggled and did a loose-jointed two-step. 'That's the way to talk! See him in hell with lead in his belly. You're taller right off the old hide, Joe.'

The liquor was working on him. It prevented him from sorting his thoughts. Noise of the place came in waves. He bought Two-Bit another drink and got outside. He wanted to see Holly, but he knew that Holly didn't want to see him. He walked up Main Street until the last false-fronted building was behind him and he was on a wagon road that led through shacks on the outskirts of town and down to the black brush shadow of the Little Box Elder.

He fought mosquitoes that rose in swarms, walking until the bank sloped down and he could smell horse mint and hear the quiet movement of water flowing beneath the brush.

There he sat, getting over the alcohol, wondering if Ma really intended to sell out to North.

Ma had changed since Holly had come back from Wyoming. Joe could remember Ma when she would have unlimbered her shotgun and scorched the hide off anyone who tried to boss a Wolverton from his old range; but when the Association started cutting them down to size all she had said was, 'You can't expect to hold fifty miles of range when you don't stock more'n half of it.' And she acted strangely

21

about other things, too. About Holly. Every time she got Joe alone she'd ask him where Holly had been and who had been coming to see him. It was as though she believed all those lies people told about Holly being in with a wild bunch down in Wyoming. Lately she didn't even want Joe to stay with Holly over at the Coalbank line shanty.

At last the whisky wore off and he went back to town.

The stage was in from Miles City. It was the mud wagon tonight, with a four-horse team pulling it. Arrival of the stage was always the big event of the night in Box Elder, and men crowded the sidewalk. Joe circled by way of the street. Light was still burning upstairs in the hotel.

He walked through cottonwoods as far as the porch. All the chairs were empty now. A man off the stage came up, staggering under the weight of a portmanteau, and Joe pretended to be interested in the latigo of his bronc. When he was inside and no one else was around, Joe found the narrow buggy tracks where Ellen had turned and headed off in the direction of Barker's freight shed. He followed the tracks but stopped suddenly just beyond the corner of the long rough-board building. The rig was only a dozen or so steps away, drawn up in shadow near the windmill tank. She was sitting on the buggy floor, feet over the edge, while Holly, beside her, lounged with one shoulder against the spring seat. Joe felt awkward. If he had known, he would not have shown himself.

'Hello,' he mumbled.

Holly had shifted a trifle, his right hand making its instinctive drop toward the gun at his hip. Then he said, 'Oh, you, Joe,' and sounded relieved.

There was nothing Joe could do except walk up. He looked at the girl. She was in shadow, but her white dress gathered a sort of phosphorescence. The manner in which she sat, leaning forward, her dress pulled tightly around her legs, made her seem small.

Holly said, 'Ellen, do you know my kid brother?'

'Yes.' There was something about her voice that knocked Joe off balance. It was a young voice, not brassy like those of the women who had been cavorting at the St. Louis, and not tired out like Ma's. 'Yes, I met Joe last summer at the grove.'

It had been Fourth of July at Woodhawk's Grove on the river. He had seen her, but he had had no idea that she had ever known who he was. He had picked on a bronc in the contest and been thrown. In the dark his cheeks burned when he imagined himself sprawled on the ground with the horse kicking dirt over him while she watched.

Then he looked up and saw her eyes.

She wasn't laughing. There was something

about her that put him at his ease. She wasn't the sort who'd laugh at a man for being busted off a bronc.

He stopped near the back wheel and looked at her. She was no older than he was, though she was already a woman while he was still not man enough to grow a respectable stubble of whiskers along his jaw. Her hair was brown, drawn back, held by a ribbon, then combed out in ringlets that fell across her shoulders. Her dress was high in the waist but not drawn tightly, so that it failed to show her true slimness, yet he could tell that she was slim and small-boned. She was like her father in build, though people said she had her mother's pretty face. Joe had never seen her mother, but he had heard about her in enough bunkhouses. She had been one of the Lennet girls from Fort Benton; she had married the Major when he was past forty and then had run away with a cowboy from the Major's own Goosebill ranch, leaving Ellen when she was a child of seven or eight.

'Meeting still on?' Holly asked.

'I guess so.'

Holly had asked just to say something. The buggy was stopped at a point where they could watch the hotel. Even if it were not true that Major Eaton had driven him away from the Goosebill, Holly would not want him to find them together because it would mean trouble for Ellen. Ever since he had lost his wife,

24

Eaton had hated cowpunchers. He never let Ellen attend the country dances like most ranchers' daughters, and he had been sending her away to a girls' school in Helena every September since she was twelve.

'What's that on your breath?' Holly asked.

Joe had hoped that Holly would notice the smell of whisky. He turned, swinging his shoulders and hitching his gun belt like Holly. 'I was down at the Elkhorn. Ran across Two-Bit Johnson.'

'You'll be taking up with sheepherders next. How many shots did he spear from you?'

Ellen said, '*He* shouldn't be in a saloon.'

Joe said: 'I can go in a saloon if I want to. I'm not a kid.'

She didn't look at him after the first surprised glance, but sat leaning forward with her elbows on her knees, chin in her cupped hands, her feet placed close together on the metal step back of the front wheel. The toes of her slippers were just visible beneath her dress, and she kept her eyes on them. There was a slight smile on her lips.

The smile made Joe say: 'Well, I'm *not* a kid. I'm just as old as you are.'

She looked surprised, as though it hadn't occurred to her. Then she looked back at her toes. 'Well, *I* don't go into saloons.'

Holly said: 'Come on, Joe, don't be so ringy. Maybe you shouldn't hang around saloons if Two-Bit Johnson's the best company you can find.'

'Two-Bit's all right. He had something to tell me about the ranch. About Ma.' He hadn't intended to mention it in front of Ellen, but he didn't want her to think he'd tagged along after his big brother, and he had to have some excuse. Anyhow, that was the real reason. 'He said Ma was figuring on selling out to North.'

'How'd Two-Bit find out?'

'Brewer told him, and Garfield told Brewer. Did you hear about it before?'

'Ma said something.'

'You're not going to let her sell?' Joe cried, startled by the thought.

'It's Ma's ranch. I guess she can sell it if she wants.'

'You mean you won't stop her?'

'How can I stop her? Anyhow, I already tried.'

'Well, *I* ain't going to let her sell. I'm going back out there.' Ellen's remark that he shouldn't be in a saloon still rankled, and he went on, saying more than he would have otherwise. 'And North hadn't better ride across our ground. If he does, I'll give him more'n he was looking for.'

He glanced over and saw that Ellen was looking at him. She seemed to be a trifle frightened.

She said, 'Please don't make trouble with him.'

'I'm not afraid of North.'

26

She stood quickly and, holding her skirt so it wouldn't catch on the brake shoe, got down from the buggy. She reached for Holly's sleeve.

'Holly, he'll get into trouble. You know what North's like.'

Holly said: 'He's a Wolverton. You said yourself you couldn't talk sense to a Wolverton.'

'I think your mother's right! You ought to sell and get out of this country. Go north, along Milk River where they've thrown all that Blackfoot land back on the public domain.'

Joe said doggedly: 'North ain't running us Wolvertons out. I'm riding yonder toward the ranch.'

Holly said, 'Don't do anything foolish.' He grabbed Joe by the arm and swung him around. 'I don't want you to go tangling with North nor any of those eighty-a-month punchers he's been bringing up from Miles, d' you understand? I ain't taking you home to Ma roped over the back of a horse.'

'I'll take care of myself.'

Holly looked him in the eyes and said: 'All right. You can drift back to the ranch without me, if you like. See you at the line shack in a couple of days.'

Joe returned to the hotel and sat out front until he heard the clump of boots moving downstairs from the meeting. He got up then, and from the shadow at one side of the porch saw them drift by twos and threes to the bar.

Ellen had been watching and now she drove up to wait. She smiled at him but neither spoke. He had an idea she was a little bit scared of her dad.

North walked out, saw her, and stood with his hat in his hand, one elbow against the front buggy wheel, to talk. The Major appeared in the door a minute later. He said, 'Cray, is that my daughter out there?' North answered Yes and the Major came outside, trying to see through the darkness. 'Ellen, didn't you hear me say that we were staying in town tonight?'

She said, 'I thought we were going back to the ranch.'

'Why, girl, you know better than that. Come down from that buggy. I'll have one of the boys take it around to the stable.' He waited for her. 'Where have you been all night?'

'Out at Sisty's.' She walked to the porch, lifting the hem of her dress to keep it from catching the slivery floor.

The Major gave her a long scrutiny, probably recalling that Holly had left the meeting hours before. He said, 'How is Sisty?' and opened the door for her.

Joe couldn't hear Ellen's answer. He stayed in the shadow and watched North cross the yard with his heavy strides and disappear up the street. He followed in time to see him turn in at the Bonanza Bar.

After a quarter of an hour North left the Bonanza with Ned Garfield and a third man, mounted, and rode away, taking the south road toward the Wolverton home ranch. Joe started after them. He rode easily; at dawn he saw them far ahead, crossing the benchland that separated Gros Ventre Creek from the Missouri River badlands. At noon they dropped from sight along the creek bottoms a couple of miles from the Wolverton home ranch.

Ned Garfield and the third man were seated beneath the pole awning on the west side of the house when he rode up. He unsaddled and turned his bronc in the corral.

Old Hap Williams, the only puncher still on the Wolverton payroll, was inside the blacksmith shop. He scarcely ever carried a gun, but he had his old Army forty-four strapped around him today.

'Creighton North inside talking to Ma?' Joe asked.

Hap nodded. 'Going up there?'

'Yes.'

'You be careful o' him. Be careful of that fellow outside, too. Know who he is? That's Ned Garfield.'

'Yes, I know.'

He walked across bare-beaten yard, trying to look casual under Garfield's scrutiny. Garfield was little more than Holly's age, perhaps twenty-five, round-faced and good-looking. Only his eyes marked the killer, and perhaps that was only because Joe was trying to read 'killer' in them.

'Hello, Joe,' Garfield said, moving himself and taking his cigarette from his lips. 'We saw you bringing up behind. Waited for you but you slowed down too much.'

He wondered if Garfield was accusing him of being a coward, but there was nothing like that in his face.

'My bronc was played out,' he said.

'Couldn't figure it was you for quite a stretch. Thought you'd be with your brother. But I guess you two have to cover a lot of country.' Garfield had a slow New Mexican drawl, an easy grace in his speech, in his movements. It was easy to imagine him whipping out his ivory-stocked forty-five with a deft swing of arm and shoulder, but it was not so easy to imagine him a killer. Garfield jerked his head at the small, rusty-complexioned man beside him. 'You acquainted with Jack Noe? He's riding for us now.'

They shook hands. Joe could hear Ma talking inside. Her voice was deep, almost like a man's, but tired, as though she'd been beat out by the country. Then North said something. The sound of his voice brought that tight feeling inside Joe's abdomen again; and his face must have shown it, because both Garfield and Noe were looking at him.

He strode inside, letting the screen door crack shut behind him.

'Joe, is that you?' his mother called.

He said, 'Yes,' and clumped through to the front room.

North had been roosting on the edge of the big plank table. He moved away and turned after the manner of a man who doesn't like to have someone at his back. He seemed taller and rangier than ever beneath the low ceiling. He spoke, calling Joe by name, and through a tight throat Joe managed to answer him.

Joe's mother sat in a straight chair, her hands folded in her lap. She was a big woman, strong as a man, and for twenty years she'd done a man's work, sometimes holding the ranch together for months on end while Clay Wolverton was in Miles for one of his sprees.

She said, 'Joe, I been giving thought to selling the ranch.'

Joe took a deep breath. He wanted to say that he'd see North in hell before selling the Winged W to him. He wanted to say it to his face just as he'd said it to old Two-Bit in the Elkhorn saloon. When he had walked through the door, he had felt almost man enough to face North that way, but now he felt empty and sick. He tried to meet North's eyes. He knew he couldn't. He knew North would see how scared he was. He wanted to crawl behind the stove and hide like a whipped dog. He was glad when Ma started to talk.

'We been offered a good price. We could take the money and go up on Milk River where they threw open that reservation land.

That is, we *could* if you thought you'd be up to running a beef spread in the teeth of those Blackfeet war parties.'

He knew what she was doing. She was trying to make it sound like he needed more guts to face the Blackfeet than to stay and face North. The Blackfeet stole a few cows, but they weren't as bad as the rustlers just over the rim in the badlands.

He said, 'I ain't going to Milk River.'

'Great Western's offered to buy our beef at the Chicago price and assume all our debts. It's not something to turn down without looking into.'

'*I* ain't looking into it.'

'Joe!' He could tell by her eyes that she was about ready to cry. He'd seen her cry a couple of times, and it had torn him worse than physical pain.

He set his jaw doggedly and said, 'We ain't selling to Great Western.'

He was scared he'd go too far. He unbuckled his gun belt, wrapped it around the holstered Colt, walked to the bedroom door, and tossed it inside on his bunk. It was ordinary enough for a man to take off his gun in the house, but he'd done it knowing North couldn't force him into drawing. He turned back from the door, feeling yellow and ashamed.

North spoke, maintaining a steely control over his voice. 'You said you wouldn't sell to

Great Western. You mean you'd sell to somebody else but not us?'

Joe wanted to stand up to him and say: 'Yes, that's what I mean. We're not getting run off the range. Not by you or Garfield or twenty more of your kind.' But all he could do was mutter, 'I mean we ain't selling.'

'Joe!' his mother said.

He was so excited it was difficult for him to stand in one place. He felt his lips trembling. He was afraid he'd break down and cry. To keep from it, he shouted:

'No, you ain't running us out of the country! Maybe you think you were pretty smart when you got Major Eaton and that tinhorn Association of his to vote us off the Squawhammer, but you ain't running us off Coalbank Creek.'

'You're not being run out!' North's voice stopped him like the cut of a whiplash. Fury had mounted in North's face. It looked hollow, as it had the night before, above the Stockman's Hotel, and his shoulder muscles stretched the blue material of his shirt. 'You may think you're a pretty smart button, giving me that kind of talk. Well, listen. I'll tell you once and that's all. I've taken all your lip I'm going to. I know what you've been peddling around the country, you and that long-riding brother of yours. It's going to stop. Do you hear me?'

Ma sprang to her feet and backed toward

33

the corner where the shotgun was leaning. 'You're not talking that way to my family inside my own house.'

North saw her reaching for the gun and pivoted, accidentally struck the table with his hip, and almost knocked off the coal-oil lamp that was sitting on it.

'Keep away from that gun!'

There was a thud of boots from outside, and Garfield cut the light from the door. He saw what was going on and stopped. He had half drawn but now he slid the gun back.

Ma shouted: 'The gun's bought and paid for. You call my boy a long rider once again and I'll turn you so the hair side's in!'

'I didn't come here to fight with women and kids. You ought to know that. I'm trying to settle this thing peacefully. You understand what I'm talking about? I'm trying to settle it peacefully.'

For just a moment Ma had been the same woman Joe had known before Clay died. Then it was over and she was saying in her beat-out voice, 'I won't sell if my boys don't want me to.'

North said, 'That's your answer?' He watched her for several seconds, then put his hat on, pulled it down hard, and strode outside.

Joe stood by the window and watched them ride away cross-country, toward the Coalbank Hills. He turned back to the table where Ma sat, staring across the room.

She said: 'Licked. Euchred, that's what dad used to say.'

'I suppose we wouldn't have been licked if we'd sold out to him!'

'You don't know what you're saying, Joey.'

'I'll see him in hell with lead in his belly before letting him have this place. I'd rather ride bareback on a mule and herd sheep.'

'I'm so sick of listening to that talk. I heard so much of it and I'm so tired of it. I wish I'd never seen this ranch. I wish I'd never seen Montana Territory, or any place where they burn letters on a cow and claim all the land they think they can shoot another man off from.'

'Ma, I didn't—'

'Oh, it ain't you. Ain't your fault. It's the way you was brought up. It's my fault. And Holly's.' There was bitterness in the way she pronounced Holly's name. 'Honest to Joab, I look at you and wonder what'll become of you. You look more like Holly and act more like him every day.'

Joe laughed. It pleased him to be compared with Holly.

She said, 'I want you to keep away from Holly and his no-account friends!'

He tilted his head back and grinned with one eye partly closed, the way Holly always did. 'Don't worry about him. He'll come out all right. He'll show North a thing or two before he's through, Holly will.'

She got up without saying any more and started poking inside the big Pittsburgh coal stove.

CHAPTER THREE

In the morning Joe hitched a team of broncs to the buck-board, tied his appaloosa saddlehorse on the tailboards, and set off for Coalbank line shack.

It had rained during the night, and sunshine was very hot through the washed atmosphere. It made him feel good to get away from the house, away from Ma, jouncing along the rough benchland trail. It wasn't that he didn't like Ma. It wasn't that at all. It was just that he had the feeling that she watched him all the time and was ready to disapprove of what he did. It wasn't like that when he lived with Holly. Even when he did what Holly told him, he felt that he was having his own way, making up his own mind. You never had to explain yourself to Holly, either. Holly always understood just how a fellow felt.

Joe kept the buckboard rolling for hours, letting the team take its own speed while the sun climbed and dried off the wet spots left by recent rains. The country was green that year, with stretches of grass, miles in length, that grew to a horse's knees, so that small ranchers like Stellingworth and Newhall, who fed their stock in the winter, could cut hay anywhere.

He watered his team at a sinkhole in Wing Coulee and then entered a country of little hills, the road winding and slowly rising toward a rocky spine of the country known as the Coalbank because of the strips of brownish lignite that cropped out along its flanks.

It was early afternoon when he sighted the line shack, a twelve by twelve shanty of cottonwood logs with a pole-and-dirt roof standing above the brush and muddy trickle of Whiterock Creek. Spring weeds had taken root in the dirt; some of them were wild peas blooming bright yellow.

As he came closer he could see that Holly wasn't there. The corral gate was down and the ax was still stuck in the chop log. When Holly chopped kindling, he always just dropped the ax wherever he happened to be.

He unhitched, hobbled the team, turned the appaloosa inside the corral. Then he carried his sack of grub to the house.

A big red steer had pushed the door open and got inside, searching for shade. Now, walleyed from fright, he lunged around, smashing the plank furnishings. His horns were so wide they had to be edged through the door, and it took Joe ten minutes to get him outside. Because of its dark red color, he thought that it was one of North's steers from over the ridge, but since it carried the D bar H of Drumheller, it was evidently one of those that Holly had contracted to take on shares. He cleaned manure off the dirt floor, sluiced it out with water from the spring, built a fire in the little sheet-metal prospector's stove, and cooked himself a dinner of salt pork and doughgods. He still had five hours before sundown, so he saddled and rode the ridge country, chasing back some Wolverton stock that had drifted to the Great Western side.

On his way back, as he was turning toward the corral, he saw a flash high in the rocks and knew that someone with field glasses was watching him.

He overcame the desire to pull up and look. The flash came from a quarter-mile off, but at that distance a man with good glasses could read the expression on his face. He kept riding, entered the corral, pulled off the saddle and bridle, and carried them to the shed. There, beyond view, he crouched on his heels and watched from a crack between the poles.

The ridge rose in a series of rocky pitches sparsely covered by grass, snakeweed, and juniper. Higher up, where the glass had flashed, gray-white sand rock stood in cliffs and pillars. There were many places a man could hide and camp for a week without being detected. He rolled a cigarette, licked it into shape, lighted it, all without taking his eyes off the rocks. Sunset faded. He had long ago finished his cigarette. It occurred to him that the man might get suspicious if he remained longer in the shed, so he walked to the house, an uncomfortable, itchy feeling between his shoulder blades.

Inside, he cooked and ate supper without lighting the bacon-grease lamp. When it was dark, before the moon rose, he slid through the back window with his rifle, hunted shadow until the brush hid him, and followed a draw that gashed deeply into the ridge. When the moon rose, he was crouched in a clump of scrub pine, looking down on the rocks from a distance of two hundred yards.

He waited for hours without seeing anything, fell asleep, and awoke stiff and aching from the early morning cold. Dawn was approaching when he got back to the cabin. He propped the door shut and finished his sleep on the bunk.

By daylight it was easy to believe that the shine had been nothing but a quartz crystal or a bottle someone had thrown uphill from the trail. He thought about it occasionally, but in the days following it ceased to bother him.

One night a sound brought him up from his blankets, his hand instinctively finding the rifle beside him. He sat for a few seconds with his bare legs over the rail of the bunk. He owned no watch, and there was not light enough to read one by if he had, but he sensed that it was late, some time between midnight and dawn.

He listened, scarcely breathing, heard the *click-clack* of hoofs on creek gravel, a voice, a scrap of laughter. He took a deep breath, relieved by the thought that it was Holly. It was often like that with Holly: a night arrival, a joke, a parting by the corral with men Joe never saw except for their shadows, single-filing away in the night.

He got up, walked barefoot and trouserless to the door. There were at least a dozen men on the far side of the corral. He could see their movements, mixed with light and moon shadow, but he heard no sound of Holly's voice. It occurred to him that they were North's men, those double-pay punchers he'd been bringing up from the cattle-war country in Wyoming. His rifle was inside, leaning against the wall. He groped for it, found it, worked the lever to bring a cartridge into the magazine. Then, with his thumb hooked over the hammer, he stepped outside, remaining close, covered by the thin strip of shadow beneath the pole eaves of the house.

The men had moved along, horses splashing the shallow trickle of creek. One of them dismounted, climbed over the corral, and slid inside, heels first, with a jingle of spurs. Joe's appaloosa, alarmed, started around the circle at a gallop.

Joe realized they were taking his horse. His hands froze on the gun, with the stock against his shoulder. But he checked the impulse to fire and shouted, 'Hey, down there!'

They had heard him and were listening. Then one of them rode at a slow, single-footing pace around the corral and headed toward the cabin.

He had a lean slouched body that gave with each movement of the horse, after the manner of one who had spent more time in the saddle than out of it. He held the reins in both hands, his elbows out, advertising that he had no intention of going for his gun—or guns, for the moonlight made a dull shine on two of them, one on each hip. The cartridges in his crossed belts must have weighed five pounds. There was a carbine in his saddle scabbard, too. Apparently he was ready for trouble. He kept peering into the darkness, and finally, when half the distance was covered, made out Joe's form beside the door.

Joe, realizing he had been seen, said, 'What d' you want?'

'Point that damn' Winchester someplace else. It might go off.'

Joe froze the sights on him. 'You come far enough!' The man eased back on the reins and stopped. The animal was blowing a little, and even by moonlight Joe could see the dark sweat streaks on his bay coat. He said, 'I asked what you wanted.'

'Where's Holly?'

'He ain't here.'

'Hasn't been here tonight?'

'That's none of your business.' He still thought that they were North's men.

'Who are you? Joe?'

'Yeah.'

'What you so ringy about? We ain't looking to trouble you. If we did, we'd have come up from behind and got you in the house. Come on, now, and point that gun away.'

Joe lowered it a few degrees. His right hand was clenched so hard around the throat of the stock that he had a hard time opening his fingers. The stranger, reassured but still wary, nudged his horse and rode the rest of the distance. He lowered his arms and, as he turned, the moon struck his face. He was about thirty-five, dehydrated by riding and by the climate, narrow-faced, with a high-ridged nose.

'So you're Joe!' he said, smiling with one side of his mouth. 'I'd of known you anywhere. Got a face just like Holly. Better lookin', maybe. Bet you're hell among the yearlin's, just like he is. Ain't he been here atall?'

'No. I don't know where he is. What do you want of him?'

'Just old friends. Late at night, but that's no never mind. Never too late for old pards like Holly and me. Knew him in Dakota and down in Wyoming, too. We been through the old Hole-in-the-Wall, Holly and me. Wanted especially to see him tonight. One of our horses went lame. We're taking that

42

appaloosa. I know Holly wouldn't mind.'

'That's *my* saddlehorse. You'll leave him alone.'

'I'm sorry, Joe, but we're takin' the appaloosa. And don't try bringing that rifle bar'l up, because I wouldn't want anything to happen to Holly's kid brother.'

Other men had ridden up through the shadow of creek brush. They'd caught the appaloosa now and were swapping saddles. Someone had ridden around the horse shed and was jogging that way, alert and tall, with his head up, a rifle across the pommel.

He called, 'Art, you having some trouble?'

'I'm having no trouble. This is Holly's brother.'

Hearing him called 'Art,' Joe knew who he was. He was Art Gamey, a rustler who was supposed to have a stronghold down in the wilds of the badlands. He'd heard that horses from as far away as Dakota, the Big Bow in Canada, and the Flathead could sometimes be found in Gamey's corral, though just where in the unexplored thousand square miles of badland cliffs and coulees it was located few men knew, or would admit if they did.

Art Gamey said, 'If Holly comes, you tell him I was here.'

'Who are you? Art Gamey?'

'Yes, I'm Gamey.' He laughed at the glimpse he had of Joe's expression. 'Hold on, kid! You don't think we're rustling that horse?'

Joe cried: 'You're taking him, aren't you? What in hell do you call it if it ain't rustling?'

'Just a favor. You'll get him back. Either him or a better one. That's a promise, kid, and I never back water on a promise. One of these mornings you'll come out of this wickiup and find a steed that can run your spotty-rumped Injun pony until his belly drags.'

Somebody called, 'Let's get to drifting, Art.'

The corral bar was down and a man rode out on the appaloosa. It made Joe sick to lose him. He'd always liked the horse. He'd broken him himself and taught him to nibble at the hip pocket of his levis for pieces of brown hard sugar. He didn't believe what Gamey said about bringing a better horse in return. Rustlers were all alike. You couldn't take their word any more than you could a tinhorn's.

They were away from the coral now and had swung around between the creek and the far bank to wait for Gamey. They started to argue about something. One of the men spoke a warning. There was a momentary, excited milling of horses. Then one of the men cut loose with his rifle. A streak of powder flame was visible against the dark underside of the creek bank; the bullet pinged as it glanced from rocks high up, along the hillside, and echoes rushed back like a rapid series of handclaps. Several seconds passed. Answering shots came in a volley, with flame marking the positions uphill, perhaps 150 yards away, where the trail dropped over some reefs from the southwest.

Joe knew that Gamey had been on a horse raid and that the others were Association men who had come cross-country to cut their trail just before it entered the badlands.

A horse squealed, wounded or bullet-burned. He crashed through brush, pawed and scrambled his way up twelve feet of almost horizontal creek bank, was silhouetted, riderless, for a second before he galloped away in more brush over the crest. Gamey's men fought back from the corrals and in cover of the bank. One group of them went down the bottoms with a clatter and splash while bullets from above dug the creek gravel and made ripping sounds through brush.

Joe had been stunned by the suddenness of the onslaught. It did not occur to him that he was in danger. He moved back, got his Winchester, worked the lever through force of habit, and ejected the cartridge he had already loaded into the barrel. He saw it bound to rest, gleaming brassily in the moonlight. When he leaned forward to retrieve it, a bullet whipped past so close he could feel the wind of its passage. He instinctively continued his motion and fell face foremost on the ground. He rolled over, swapped ends in getting to his hands and knees, and dived through the door as a second bullet followed him. He kept going and stopped face down on the earthen floor.

Much of the mud and grass chinking had fallen from beneath the logs and just over his head was an opening large enough to admit the barrel and sights of the gun. He thrust it through as far as the forearm, spotted a flash of powder sixty or seventy yards up the ridge, and pressed the trigger. The kick felt good against his shoulder. He kept levering the rifle and firing until the magazine was empty. He got up and groped along the bench to where he had dropped his cartridge belt the night before.

His rifle was an old timer, a forty-four, made to take the same cartridge as his Colt. The rifling had been shot from its barrel, and every time it exploded there was a squirt of smoke and burned powder from the breech bolt. He hadn't noticed it much in the excitement of shooting, but he did now. One side of his face smarted and he was half blind. Powder smoke was raw in his throat. He began coughing and couldn't stop. Bullets now were whipping like angry hornets through the cabin blackness. He got down on his face, still coughing, and lay behind the thick sill log. After a while the smoke cleared away. He could smell bullet-pulverized wood. He pulled his belt down beside him, drew cartridges from its loops and fed them through the spring opening of the magazine.

Four or five minutes had passed. They had stopped blasting the cabin now. He raised himself enough to peep through the chinking.

Some of Gamey's men had been pinned down at one side of the corrals. Now they made it to the horse shed. He could hear the muffled concussions of their guns inside. Others he could see beyond the creek, leading horses along, protected by the undercut bank. Slowly the shooting petered out. Minutes went by. It was so quiet he could hear the ring of crickets, the quiet murmur of creek water across stones. Then the gunfire burst out again, perhaps half a mile down the draw. It lasted five or six minutes, then quieted again. After a very long wait he could hear the popping of guns far away in the badlands.

CHAPTER FOUR

Dawn came, a gray, diffused light from the horizon. Fading the moon and stars, its first effect was to make things seem darker than before, then it commenced washing out the heavy shadows that covered the corrals and the creek.

Joe had been so long in one place that he felt paralyzed. He was cold and stiff. He had never got around to putting his pants and boots on. He limped about, restoring circulation to his body, dressed, got the rifle in the crook of his arm, and edged into the

47

doorway. When nothing happened, he walked warily toward the corrals.

A dead man lay face down on white, alkali-coated gravel at the far side of the creek.

Joe drew up, then fell back a step. It wouldn't have bothered him so much while the fight was on. Now the events of the night seemed like a nightmare, but the dead man was reality. He'd been hungry a moment before but now he was sick, and he didn't want to look at food again, ever. He felt hot, with a clammy sweat on his forehead. He wished he could get on a horse, ride into the wind, and never see the line shack nor that sweep of corral and creek bottom again. He stood for several minutes with dawn growing at his back, then, getting a hold on himself, walked down the slope, jumped the creek, and stood over the dead man.

He was a stranger, and that helped: a young man, slim and narrow-hipped. A bullet had hit him in the center of the breast, gone straight through, and probably killed him instantly. An undented hat lay a few steps away. He wore chaps, heavy leather ones with silver conchal down both wings. You sometimes saw men coming up from the brush country of the southwest with chaps like that, though they generally swapped for chokebore angoras when winter started freezing their legs the shape of a horse.

Joe stood over him, wondering what he

ought to do. He'd have to bury him. There was a shovel in the shed. He had leaned his rifle against a stack of quaking-asp corral poles and started away to fetch the shovel when he heard the crash of horses through brush and spun around to see riders cresting a shoulder of ground through buffalo-berry bushes. There were six of them, headed by Ned Garfield, and they had rifles across their saddles. North's men. He should have been scared of Garfield. He should have been more scared of Garfield than he was of North, but it didn't hit him that way. At least, he was no longer alone with the dead man.

They covered the distance with their broncs at a wary wolf trot. He recognized more of them—Jack Noe, Dick Dean, and heavy-jawed Alvis Brewer.

Garfield led them on a zigzag path down the steep bank, splashed through mud and shallow water up the creek. Then his blue roan bronc saw the dead man and pivoted. Garfield quieted him with a firm rein, saying, 'Easy, bronc, easy.' He tilted his head at the dead man and asked Joe, 'Who is it?'

'Never saw him before.'

Alvis Brewer laughed with a contemptuous jut of his jaw and said, 'I'll *bet* you never!' He got down from his horse stiffly, pulled his pants away from his legs, and limped over to where the man was lying. He had a chew of tobacco in his cheek. He spat across the gravel.

Sight of the dead man had put a chill even on this rough gunman bunch, and feeling it, he took the opportunity to show that he didn't share it. He worked the toe of one boot under the dead man's breast and with a hard lift rolled him to get a full view of his face.

Garfield asked, '*You* know him?'

'Saw him at Musselshell a while back. He was drunk and beating his chest. Called himself the Kiowa Kid.'

Garfield turned his back on Brewer and the dead man and spoke to Joe. 'Any more of them holed up around here, kid?'

'No.'

'You better tell the truth.'

'I am! I ain't seen anybody in two hours.'

Garfield nodded and dismounted, smooth and supple despite his time in the saddle. 'Reckon we'll light here. They'll be along. They're just wasting good ca'tridges down yonder. Take half the cavalry in the territory to run anybody down in those badlands. You got a spring here, Joe? I ain't drunk anything betten'n cow-track water since yesterday mawnin'.'

They sprawled around and waited while the sun came up and drove morning chill from the air.

'They're coming,' Jack Noe said from his place near the corral. 'Leading that gray horse of Pete McGuffy's.'

Brewer said, 'It *was* Pete they knocked over,

50

then.'

Joe had been sitting with his back to the heap of aspen poles. He rocked forward to his feet. Pete was Guff McGuffy's half-breed son. He liked Pete; everybody did, even though he got drunk and mean every time he was close to a whisky bottle.

Jack Noe climbed the corral and waved his hat, shouting, 'All clear!' and the main group of fourteen Association riders dropped down from the northeast. They were led by Creighton North.

North was astraddle a heavy-legged bay horse. He saw Joe, swung down, dropped the bridle, and walked stiff-legged, stabbing his boot heels across the hoof-punched, drying mud. He jerked his head at Joe and asked Garfield, 'Find him here?'

'Yeah.'

'Holed up in the shack?'

'No, he was here, looking at the dead man. Notice we got ourselves a dead man?'

North didn't bother to answer, but Alvis Brewer thought it was funny and tossed his head back with a heavy-throated laugh.

North, still looking at Joe, talking to Garfield, said, 'See anything of his brother?'

'I reckon the kid was here alone.'

A twist of North's lips showed that the gunman's words irked him. 'What makes you so damned sure of that?'

'Maybe you shouldn't bother to ask.'

The others had ridden down. Joe knew most of them. They were from Great Western, the Goosebill, and McGuffy's 77, all except old Billy Buzzard, who didn't have much to gain one way or the other and who probably had just come along for the ride.

Alf Koenig asked who the dead man was and Brewer said: 'Rustler. Called himself the Kiowa Kid.'

'Makes two we got.'

North said: 'Egg suckers! The big rattlesnakes all got away.' Then for the first time he addressed Joe. 'All right, Wolverton, not that it'll be news to anybody, but who else was in the gang?'

'I don't know.'

'Who'd we jump down here at the corral— *besides* your brother?'

'Holly wasn't here!' He had to raise his voice to override the tremble in it. 'I don't know who any of 'em were!'

North laughed, his mouth twisted down, with a hard jerk of his head and shoulders. The laugh, better than words, named Joe a little liar. 'All right, kid. Don't carry it any farther. You haven't got your mother's skirts to hide in to-day.'

'I tell you I don't know who they were. It was dark. I couldn't see 'em down by the corral any more'n you could. I was asleep up there at the shack when—'

'You lie to me again, and I'll—'

52

Koenig cut in, 'Let him tell his story, Cray.'

North was leader of the group; more than half the men were on his payroll, and he didn't like being interfered with. However, Koenig represented the Goosebill, so he had to give in.

Joe fought back the excitement in him. His fists were doubled at his sides, his jaw jutted, and he appeared to be cocky and swaggering. 'I was shacked up here ever since getting back from Box Elder. Been riding line. I woke up along after midnight and heard somebody at the corrals. Whole pack of 'em. Never saw 'em before. They was saddling my appaloosa. Then the shooting started and I hid inside the house. That's every bit I know.'

North said, 'When I rode over the bridge up yonder, somebody had been at the house and was riding back to the corrals. Who was *that*?' He waited, then shouted, 'Who was it, your brother?'

'No, it wasn't! It was Art Gamey.'

'Thought you didn't know who *any* of them were.'

He felt trapped. 'I didn't. I guessed he was Art Gamey. He came up here telling me to stay clear and not cause any ruckus about the appaloosa.'

North barked, 'Where's Holly?'

'I don't know.' He was almost crying. 'I told you already. I haven't seen him since that Association meeting in Box Elder.'

'You're lying.'

North came forward. Joe retreated instinctively. The corral rammed his back.

North said: 'You might as well admit it. It was Holly. I could see who it was.'

'It wasn't. He wasn't here. He ain't any cattle rustler. You know damn' well he ain't a cattle rustler. You just want to make him out one so you'll have an excuse to shove us off the rest of our range like you did off'n the—'

North moved with the quickness of a big cat. He feinted with his open left hand, and when Joe instinctively moved aside, the right hand struck him. North hadn't doubled his fist. He struck with the hand flat, fingers together, a chopping blow across the side of the neck. It snapped Joe's head to one side as though he had hit the end of a hangman's rope.

He sagged to his knees. His eyes were baffled, out of focus, and his mouth was open. North seized him by the front of his shirt. He jerked him upright, held him up with legs still limp. Then he struck him repeatedly with the palm and back of his hand.

'Lie to me again!' he said hoarsely. 'Go ahead, lie to me! Lie to me!'

'All right, North!' McGuffy said.

North kept striking him. He'd held his fury against the Wolvertons for days and months, and now that it had slipped its leash it was hard for anything else to get through to his brain.

'North!' McGuffy cried.

He stopped. The effort had winded him. He sucked his lungs full three or four times. Then he dumped Joe on the ground and hitched up his trousers.

'Maybe he's the one that killed your boy, Guff.'

Guff said, 'I don't guess he is.'

'You that sure about his brother?'

'No, I'm not sure. I don't suppose I'll ever know who killed Pete. But it ain't going to do any good to slap the kid around.'

'Little snake or big snake, I believe in getting the whole den. He was there in the shack. You heard him admit it. We all saw that rifle shooting between the logs.'

'We were shooting at the shack too. That don't prove anything.'

'Maybe it doesn't prove anything that that rustler outfit rode straight here after we busted up the raid.'

'I ain't on their side, North. You ought to have sense enough to see that.'

They all stood there, watching Joe get his wits about him. A red welt had appeared at the side of his neck. His hair was strung over his face, and his baffled eyes shone through it. He got into a sitting position, one hand propped behind him, and rubbed the other back and forth across his face. The inside of his mouth had been cut by his own teeth. Blood ran from his lips, and his hand smeared it around from ear to ear. It looked funny to some of the men, who laughed.

Alvis Brewer, still chuckling, dipped his big hat into the creek, walked over, and poured the water in a stream that struck Joe on the head and spattered in all directions. The water, that early in the morning, was cold, and it shocked him out of his bewilderment. He writhed back and forth, trying to get out of the way while Brewer kept pouring; he cursed and then coughed up some of the water that he had drawn into his lungs.

'Lay off, Brewer,' Alf Koenig said.

Brewer took orders from no one but North, and he managed to show that in his attitude. He tossed away the final bit of water and said, 'Don't you think he needed some cleanin' up?'

Joe kept cursing them, cursing and half crying: 'I'll kill you. I'll get a gun and kill the whole yellow-streaked bunch of you.'

Brewer drew his Colt and offered it, butt first, with the obvious intention of jerking it back when Joe reached for it. 'Here, kid, you can't gunfight with your lip.'

'Lay off him!' Koenig shouted.

Alvis Brewer spun the gun with a deft movement and rammed it back in the holster. Koenig dismounted, then, and walked across to Joe.

'We ain't blaming you, Joe. You nor your Ma, neither one. But you see how it looks for you. This isn't the first time they came here.

We know that. We had a man watching from up the ridge. Been there watching off and on for a month. Those rustlers, Gamey's outfit, they been here before.'

'How can us Wolvertons help that? The badlands are crawling with long riders and rustlers. There's bands of Blackfeet and Cheyennes down there, even, on the jump from the agency. You expect us Wolvertons to watch the whole rim from here to the Goosebill and chase 'em back? If you want 'em cleaned out, why don't you tell it to the law? Let Tripp and Slager do it. You elected 'em.'

'Gamey doesn't ride right up to the Goosebill house.'

'You ain't there all alone like I am here.'

'Joe, listen. I know how you feel. About your brother, that is. But it'll do you no good to try and protect him. Gamey and his gang was on a horse raid, and we chased them all the way from Rosebud Coulee. They tried to lose us crossing the beaver dams on Dolly Creek, then they swung back over the ridge and came straight here. They were after fresh horses. They knew the horses would be waiting for them.'

'Only horse in the corral was my appaloosa, and that's all they took. I had my gun out and tried to stop 'em, but what could I do against that bunch? I notice you fellows hid in the rocks. You didn't tackle 'em all alone.'

'They just took the one horse?'

'That's all.' Joe looked around at their faces, at Koenig, and Guffy, and old Billy Buzzard. They didn't believe him. Not even Billy Buzzard.

'Oh, the hell with it,' North said. He walked down to look at the dead man, turned and came back.

Jack Noe said, 'Here comes somebody.'

Joe, fearing it might be Holly, climbed the corral to see. The rider was unrecognizable with sun glare around him, but it wasn't Holly.

'Chad Newhall,' Koenig said.

Newhall's place stood on one of the flats of Thirty-Mile Coulee not far to the east. He rode up, looking them over, nodding to one and another without saying anything, nor did he say anything when he saw the dead man.

North asked, 'Who you looking for, Chad?'

'That's what I ought to ask.' He noticed Joe's face. 'You been having the nosebleed?'

Joe didn't say anything.

Newhall lighted his burned-out cigarette. 'I heard some shooting; thought I'd head over this way. What was it?'

Koenig said: 'Gamey's bunch from the badlands. They were after fifty-sixty head of saddle stock off Guff's range. We chased 'em here. They were getting fresh horses at the corral.'

Newhall gave him a long look. 'You mean Joe had fresh horses waiting for them?'

'I mean Holly did.'

'Holly! Oh, hell, Holly couldn't of been here.'

North snapped, 'How in hell you so sure of that?'

'He was at my place last night. We played cards till near onto midnight. Then he took out for Ma's. Jennie heard shooting and I got up, but it was a long ways off. Sounded like down in the badlands. I got kind of worried about Joe and came over to see if there'd been any trouble. I and my wife sometimes get worried about Joe, him camping here at the edge of the badlands with Art Gamey on one side of him and North on the other.'

Newhall smiled a little when he said it, but it wasn't exactly a joke. A small rancher, he too was feeling the press of the big interests.

A couple of the boys laughed, and that stung North more than Newhall's words. He said, 'Why in hell are you so interested in clearing the Wolvertons?'

'Now, hold on. Maybe I got the wrong idea. What you out for—to run out the Wolvertons, or stop all this horse rustling that's been going on?'

North shouted, 'I listened to enough of that talk, and—'

'All right, Cray, then you're out to stop the rustlers. Tell you how we'll settle the argument. Ride over to my house and ask my family. I'm one man that's got plenty of witnesses.'

Alf Koenig spoke in a conciliatory tone. 'We're not doubting you. You say he was there, why, he was there. I, for one, am damned glad to hear it.'

CHAPTER FIVE

They buried the dead man somewhere on the hillside. Joe didn't know where and he didn't want to know.

When they were gone, Newhall asked, 'North beat you up?'

Sympathy almost made Joe bawl again. He fought it back by jutting his chin and saying, 'I'll get him alone sometime. I'll catch up with him when he ain't backed by that bunch of gunmen. And when I do, I'll put a bullet in him. I'll shoot his damn' head off.'

'Don't make that kind of talk when folks can hear you.'

'If you think anybody's going to slap me around without—'

'You take my advice and forget about it. And don't tell Holly too much, either. He'll just get himself in trouble. You better come on over to the house with me and eat some decent cooking.'

'No, I'm going to stay here. I expect Holly will be around as soon as he gets wind there was a ruckus.'

He cooked breakfast. His mouth was so swollen he could hardly eat. There was a knot in the muscles of his neck and he had a hard time turning his head.

He watched for Holly all day. A thunderstorm rose in the southwest, covering the sunset, and an early lead-gray darkness settled. He fell asleep with the sound of rain dripping from the pole eaves.

He woke up with the storm cleared and the moon shining. Someone had ridden up to the corral. Half asleep, he had heard the ring of a horseshoe on stone, but it did not alarm him as it had last night. He had been wishing too much for it, wanting to see Holly. He picked up his rifle from force of habit and went to the door. A man was already walking with a spur jingle up from the corral.

Holly said, 'Hello, Joe,' in his easy voice. 'Don't you ever sleep?'

'It don't pay to sleep in this country any more.'

Holly laughed and kept walking. He had a package under his arm. There was something different about him—the hat he was wearing. It was a tan-brown Stetson that must have cost him $20.

The moon struck Joe's face then, and Holly stared at him. 'What you tangle with, a bobcat?'

'Had a little ruckus.'

'Who with?'

Joe told him about the shooting, the dead man, and the Association riders, trying to make it sound as offhand as Holly himself did when he described similar affairs in Wyoming.

But Holly wasn't smiling. His face, which had been carefree a moment before, now looked hollow beneath the cheekbones, and his eyes had become narrow and predatory.

He broke in and said, '*Who* slapped you around?'

Joe recalled Newhall's warning, but there was no way he could keep Holly from learning the truth. 'North.'

'Who was with him? Just Garfield, Brewer, and that bunch?'

'No, the whole pack of 'em.' He named them over, as many as he could remember.

'They stood and let him do it?'

'Koenig and old Guff were all right. Wouldn't of blamed Guff if *he'd* been mean. I was shooting at them from the house. Pete got killed, you know.'

'No, I didn't.' He stepped inside the house with Joe following, booted the door shut, got a burlap bag, and hung it across the window before lighting the bacon-grease dip. He unbuckled his gun and tossed it on the bunk. 'Well, what in hell does Guff expect, backing the big outfits? He ought to be with us and Newhall and Stellingworth. If they chase us out of the country, where'll he go to look for friends then? Maybe he'll write a letter to

Benjamin Harrison.'

'You don't really think they'll shove us off the range, do you?'

'I don't know. We're caught between Great Western and the Goosebill.' He winked and added, 'But we'll try to keep 'em from enjoying the job too much.'

Joe whispered, 'I'll get him some time!'

'Don't worry, kid. One of us'll catch him all even up without his hired guns. We'll hit him with lead and sing a song over him. But we won't do much talking about it beforehand, will we? Noticed it plenty times in the past—man that does the most shootin' with his mouth does the least with his gun.' He was grinning again now. He slapped Joe on the shoulder. 'Open up that package. I brought you something.'

Joe broke the string and pulled the paper off. Inside was a hat like Holly's, boots with stitched clubs and spades, and a pair of spurs—polished brass with silver star rowels and dinglebobs.

Joe had had new spurs at one time—a cheap pair from Barker's in Box Elder, but he'd never owned a hat or boots that hadn't been castoffs.

'All of it for me?'

'Sure, what the hell? You're a man now. Can't run around looking like a sheepherder. Well, aren't you going to try 'em on?'

He put on the hat, started to dent it down

the front like his old one, then decided to wear it as Holly was wearing his. His socks were old and full of holes, and it seemed a shame to wear them with the new boots, so he pulled the boots on his bare feet. He wished he had a mirror so that he could look at himself. He wondered if there was enough moonlight to see himself in the creek. He hadn't noticed before, but there was a new neckerchief, too, a flowered silk one, very thick and of a coppery greenish-black color. With it was a snap-down silver concha to hold it around his throat.

Holly did a polka step and said: '*Now* you look like something. I'd hate to trust you across the tracks in Miles now. Those fancy gals from St. Louis would kidnap you, and you'd end up with more money than you started out with.'

'Oh, hell!'

'Put on the spurs.'

He put them on and jingled around the cabin. He hoisted a heel on the plank table and drew the spur across, leaving a rowel mark. 'Wish Gamey'd bring my appaloosa back.'

'He will. Art's all right. He might stick a gun in your belly and take your poke, but he wouldn't sneak around and organize an association to do his stealing for him.' Holly felt the stove. It had long been cold. 'I'm hungry. Haven't had anything except sardines since morning.'

'Ain't you been at Ma's?'

'No.'

'Chad said you left his place for Ma's.'

'When was Chad here?'

Joe hadn't got to that part of his story. He told how everybody, even Guff and Billy Buzzard, had thought that Holly had been in on the horse raid until Chad Newhall had told them that he'd been at his house most of the night playing cards.

Holly said: 'Oh, sure. But when I pulled out I didn't go back to Ma's.'

He didn't say where he'd gone, and Joe instantly thought about Ellen Eaton. For some reason it always gave him an uneasy sensation to think of them being together. It made him go hot and cold, and to hide it he started building the fire.

After four or five minutes heat made the house uncomfortable, so Holly opened the door. He didn't show himself, though, and he still left the burlap bag over the window.

'They had somebody up on the hill, watching through glasses,' Joe said.

Holly made no comment. He waited for Joe to hand him a tin cup of coffee. Then he grinned and said, '*You* don't think I'm in with Gamey, do you?'

'Of course, I don't!' It cut Joe to think that Holly would even ask such a thing.

While Holly wolfed pancakes and bacon, Joe admired his new possessions. The hat's sweatband was branded by the Stevens Company of St. Louis, so he knew it must have come from their trading post at Musselshell. That was Stevens's closest store.

'You been all the way to Musselshell?'

'Oh, I lather hell out of a horse.'

Joe fell asleep trying to figure out where Holly had been. He couldn't sleep after sunup, so he left Holly snoring in the bunk, roped one of the broncs from the team, and rode around, watching the shadow he made with his new hat and scarf. When he got back, it was noon and Holly was still asleep. Finally Holly got up, had a bath standing ankle-deep in the creek, and shot prairie chickens for supper.

'Tomorrow,' he said to Joe, 'we'll start drifting those D bar H steers back over the ridge.'

It was dawn, cold enough for a jacket, when they started out and crossed the Coalbank. Pine grew there, with quaking asp and chokecherry in the draws. Things smelled differently in the hills, greener, with an odor of flowers a person never found in the sage country. Springs were plentiful, though many of them would go dry by August. They followed a creek terraced with beaver dams. The pools were seldom more than ten feet across, circled by brush; from above they looked like coins, flat-shining in the dawn light.

Holly said, 'If I ever built a house to live in,

I'd build it up here and not down on that dry prairie.'

It surprised Joe that Holly should think of settling down in a house.

The sun came up and grew hot on their shoulders. After the first steep slopes of the Coalbank, the country fell away in gentle hills that later graded into a rolling prairie cut by many coulees and draws, with the deepest of them, the Squawhammer, fifteen miles away. The country appeared to rise steeply beyond the Squawhammer, but it was an illusion, a telescopic effect attributable to the remarkable spring clarity of the atmosphere. Actually, the rise was many miles in scope, and so gentle a man was scarcely aware of it when he rode the freight road to Musselshell Landing. Farther on there was another cleft, much deeper, the Musselshell, and still there was no end, no real horizon. Sky and earth joined in what appeared to be a gray-purple sea with little hill ranges rising here and there like pointed islands. The illusion of a distant sea increased as the sun rose and the day became hot, with heat wave and mirage to distort the distance.

Joe remained tense for many miles, watching for North's men, but he forgot about them when the work started, working the hill ends of draws, finding here and there a critter carrying the D bar H iron.

When darkness settled, they were eight miles deep in the Great Western range, herding twenty-two steers to a coulee waterhole. They slept there and started back slowly, working coulees at the edge of the badlands and crossing the ridge with a total of fifty-five. These they scattered along Wing Coulee. Then they spent two days visiting Ma and gathering a six-horse remuda. The hunt continued in a leisurely manner through the early days of June.

One afternoon Joe was driving two D bar H steers down a draw toward the main bunch, which was being held on some flats near an abandoned trapper's shanty. He had formed the habit of watching the country, and from the side of the draw he sighted four riders moving in from the south-east. He would have kept out of view but they had seen him, so he pulled up and waited. From a quarter of a mile away he knew that one of the men was Alvis Brewer. Another proved to be Jack Petit, a dried-up graying man who'd ridden for one or another of the Musselshell outfits ever since Joe could remember. The others were strangers, cowboys.

Brewer saw who it was and came riding up with the tapaderos on his stirrups slapping at the sage clumps. 'Well, I'm damned, if it ain't the fightin' man! You don't learn very easy, do you? How many times you got to be told this is Great Western range?'

Joe was nervous, but he was not as frightened of Brewer as he was of North. He did not have any trouble looking him in the eyes and saying, 'I know what range this is.'

Petit rode up, called him by name, and with one hand on the saddlehorn and the other on the cantle turned to scrutinize the two steers that were grazing down the draw.

'They're carrying the D bar H, all right,' he said to Brewer.

'I know it's a D bar H.' He turned to Joe. 'What in hell you doing, rounding up D bar H stock? You got a representation from them in your pocket?'

'I don't need any representation paper. We got that stock on shares from Stickley, and the Association told us to come over here and chase them to our home range. That's what we been doing. North agreed to it. So what you kicking about?'

Brewer knew that already, otherwise he wouldn't have accepted the explanation. 'How many head you got grazing on our grass?'

'North knows that, too. It all came out in the Association meeting.'

'I suppose you was there.'

'Yes, I was.'

When North and Garfield weren't within listening distance, Brewer liked to act as if he were top dog. It cut his pride that this kid had been at the meeting while he'd been left to drift around Box Elder's saloons. He laughed with a mean look on his face, advertising that he put no weight on anything Joe said.

One of the punchers, a blond, well built man, returned after riding halfway to the steers and said: 'I know that brindle steer. Remember him from the beef roundup last fall. Only he wasn't branded any D bar H then. He was marked Snaky G.'

Brewer leaned forward, thrusting out his heavy jaw. 'You sure of that?'

'You can bet your fat roll I'm sure of it. I'd remember that steer anywhere.'

Petit said, 'We got a thousand brindle steers, Charley.'

'Maybe we have, but I tell you I remember that one down there. He was in our cut of the beef that the renegade rider drove over from the Musselshell roundup. There were eighty, eighty-five of them, and this brindle steer was in the bunch. He's the same one. Paul Ardle and I were joking that he looked like a gambler's dream. He's got a mark on his rump that looks like a club, and one on his flank like a spade. He's the same steer, all right.'

That was enough to convince Alvis Brewer, and he showed it by the way he spat tobacco juice and wiped his mouth on the back of his hand. But old Jack Petit just blinked and said: 'We better go easy, raising a ruckus about it. That ain't any haywire spread, the D bar H; and if we claim the steer, we're claiming they run our brand.' He slid his hat down to shade sun from his eyes. 'Anyhow, it'd take some doing to figure a Snaky G out of that.'

Charley said, 'It'd be an easy switch for a good man with a running iron.'

'Ain't any such thing as a *good* man with a running iron.'

'Look here; he could just draw out that snake on the bottom hook of the G and make a bar of it.' He swung down from his horse and with one finger traced the two brands in the dirt:

G~   ƉH

'Then all he'd need do is make the H, pluck some hairs on the D, and he'd have it.'

Petit said: 'Maybe you saw the steer someplace else. Could have been you saw him in the D bar H cut and forgot.'

Brewer said, 'Who the dirty old hell's paying you, anyhow?'

'The Great Western's paying me, but you're not doing them any favor when you get to yelling 'rustler' at an outfit like Drumheller. Maybe you don't know it, but they're big shakes north of the river. They're bigger even than Great Western.'

'We'll cut 'em down to size.' He looked back at Joe. 'Maybe they don't do their own brand running. Maybe they got an outfit on this side to doctor up a steer here and there so he'd get by the brand inspector.'

Anger made Joe's pulse hammer in his throat as it had that morning back at the line shanty before North slapped him around. He knew he should keep still, but he heard himself saying: 'I notice you don't go around by yourself accusing us Wolvertons. You always have men at your back.'

'All right, Wolverton, I'll tell you what: I'll send these boys down-coulee so we'll be all alone, just the two of us.'

'I ain't a-scared of you!'

Petit said, 'I'm having no part of this, Brewer.'

'He's man enough to carry a gun and run brands.'

'Let's let the Association decide about the brand running.'

'The Association!' Brewer spat. 'That outfit'll be cackling about it for the next twelve months. Give me twenty men of my own choosing, and I'd clean this range out in a week.' The fourth puncher had ridden down and was examining the brands. Brewer called to him: 'All right, shag 'em this way. We'll take 'em over to the boss.'

'Somebody coming,' Charley said.

Holly, riding at an easy amble, had appeared over a bulge of ground an eighth of a mile away. Brewer, watching him, became tense. He was silent during the minute it took Holly to reach them.

'Hello, Jack,' Holly said to Petit when he

was close enough to be heard without raising his voice. He nodded to Charley and to Brewer. It might have been any chance meeting, except that there was a watchfulness in his narrowed eyes. 'What's up?'

Brewer said, 'We're taking that brindle steer.'

The steer was half hidden by brush, so Holly waited until it had grazed far enough out to show the brand. 'That's a D bar H.'

'Yes, and we want North to look at it.'

'He's seen the D bar H before. He knows they're on this range. And he agreed to us driving 'em home.'

'I don't think he ever saw a D bar H like *that* before.'

Holly was slack and pleasant, but his words fell with a deadly flat sound. 'You got something bothering you? Why don't you go ahead and say it?'

Joe could feel tension like the spring of a trap bent and triggered. He gave his bronc all the bridle he wanted, drifted away. He didn't want Charley or Jack Petit behind him. His forty-four was at his hip. He itched to feel for it, to make sure he hadn't rammed it down too hard, as he sometimes did to keep it from jouncing loose. He didn't touch it, though. He knew what might happen if he moved his hand that way.

'I got guts enough,' Brewer said. 'That's a tampered brand.'

73

'Want to say who tampered it?'

'I won't say that till I know. But I'm taking him over for the boss to see.'

'You're leaving him here.'

Brewer's response was sudden. He rammed his legs stiff, standing in the stirrups, and twisted around. The butt of his gun was above his hand, so that all he had to do was to jerk it straight up from the holster. Holly appeared to slouch back and to one side. His right boot was pushed out almost horizontally. Without making much show of action, his gun was in his hand. He hesitated perhaps no more than the sixth part of a second, though it seemed long. Then the gun exploded and the heavy slug hit Brewer, smashing him back so that his seat was behind the cantle of the saddle. His horse lunged. For a moment he remained on the animal's back, gun dangling in his fingers. Then he pitched sideways, the horse leaving him. He struck the sloping ground of the draw head and shoulder first and slid for twenty feet before a tangle of sagebrush stopped him.

Joe had drawn his forty-four. The cowboy, Charley, had a gun in his hand.

Joe fired from thirty feet. He saw the cowboy twist and he thought the bullet had gone home, but it had whanged the saddle horn and glanced. The force of it, like a hammer blow, stung the horse through the tree of the saddle. He sunfished, dumped his rider on the second jump, and bucked away down the draw with his head down and empty stirrups whopping.

It was over then. No more than ten seconds had passed. The rider down-coulee had drawn his carbine from the scabbard, but he kept his distance, making no move to use it.

Holly sat, with smoke stringing from the muzzle of his forty-five, and looked down on Charley, who was sitting with both hands propped behind him, blinking and groggy.

'You're lucky to be alive,' Holly said.

Charley didn't say anything. He got to his feet, his chaps making him awkward so that he almost fell again. His hat lay near by, horse-kicked out of shape. He retrieved it, fingered dirt and sage leaves from his hair, and put it on. Then he saw Brewer's body and stopped. The sight took the guts out of him. He looked drawn and bluish around the mouth.

Holly knew at a glance that he had nothing more to fear from him, so he said, 'Go ahead and pick up your gun.'

He thought Holly intended to make him fight. His eyes traveled to the gun and back again, but he didn't move. He looked as though he were suffering from ptomaine.

Jack Petit said: 'Pick it up, Charley. Holly's got his man for supper.'

Holly said: 'He drew first. Didn't you notice?'

'Don't get hostile with me. I didn't cause you trouble.'

Charley picked up the gun by its barrel and fed it down into the holster without more than his wrist touching the butt.

Petit said, 'Well, Holly boy, what now?'

'That's up to North. If he wants me, I'll be easy to track.'

Joe became aware that he was still holding his gun; he put it back. He felt sweated out, and his mouth and throat were dry. He had hated Brewer a moment before, but now he no longer felt anything. Petit and the other two riders caught Brewer's saddle horse, lifted his body, and tried to rope it on. The horse was frightened and kept backing in a circle. They made a second try, blindfolding him, and that failed too.

Petit said, 'We'll send the wagon down after him,' and they rode away.

Holly came up beside Joe and asked, 'What was it about that brindle steer?'

'Why, that rider they call Charley claimed he knew some of his club and spade markings from the beef roundup. Said he was in with a bunch of Snaky G strays.'

'They're looking for stuff like that. Any excuse to hang it on a Wolverton. We better round up the herd and shag them down to the badlands.'

CHAPTER SIX

The coulee, which had been a gentle, grassy depression in the prairie, became a steep V when it broke into the badlands. Its sides were stratified clay and shale with an occasional layer of sandstone which jutted out to make a rim. Sage and sword grass grew where it could find root, but the big areas were only rock and dirt.

The steers were walleyed with terror at the steep, rough going. When one tried to stop, he was piled on by those behind, forced on again. At each turn where the bottom widened a trifle, a milling drag of eight or nine steers usually developed, but the two riders were on them immediately, shouting and swinging rope goads.

The coulee deepened. It became a cut whose sides were mountainous. Eagles, soaring above, made their full circles inside the walls. Sun still shone high on the rims while the bottom gathered twilight.

They entered a roughly circular area of hummocky relief about a mile in diameter, a meeting place of several coulees. Box-elder trees grew farther along, and the night breeze carried the smell of the musty manure and a mucky spring.

Holly was behind with the remuda, and Joe

pulled in to wait for him. He was sweating, and the sweat was so filled with dirt that it ran in streaks of mud down his cheeks and the sides of his neck. He wiped it off with his shirtsleeve and said: 'This is a hell of a place. How you ever expect to get 'em out again?'

'Let North worry about it.'

'It's our stock. A share of 'em, anyway.'

'In this country you own what you can hold. Anyhow, don't worry. I can get 'em out again. I know these draws like most men know their way around inside of a tin plate. You stick with me, kid. I'll show you some places you never dreamed about.'

The stock did not need driving now, with the smell of water in their nostrils. They clattered down a dry bottom and waded through mud, manure, and the greenish bones of mired animals to drink from water-filled depressions.

A footpath climbed to a trickle of clear water where Holly filled a canvas water bag. They made a fire in a bower of box elders and cooked supper.

Joe, thinking about Brewer, asked, 'You think they'll start any ruckus?'

'Don't worry about them. Those fellows aren't any more'n back at the ranch. They won't start tracking before daylight. Hell, nobody would track you into these badlands, anyhow.'

They started moving at dawn, up a coulee

that came in from the east, across a ridge, down again. Noon found them descending the side of a dry watercourse of such scope that it must, at some prehistoric time, have accommodated the whole Missouri. Beneath them were long slopes covered with talus rocks, then pillars of sandstone, and cliffs, and more talus slopes. A herd of antelope, crossing the bottom, looked as tiny as jackrabbits.

Holly reined in and opened his shirt to let wind cool the sweat from his body. When Joe rode up, he gestured below and said: 'You could spend your life riding this country and die of rheumatism before you saw more'n half of it. You ever see an elephant, Joe?'

'Sure. Saw one in the circus at Miles.'

'You wouldn't believe it, Joe, but there used to be elephants hereabouts, or something even bigger.'

'Oh, hell,' Joe said. 'Why'nt you stick with sidehill gougers?'

'This is on the level. Over yonder—oh, a hell of a long way past Painted Rock, there's a place where the wolfers used to go and dig coal. Well, they dug more'n coal out of there. They dug bones. They got a skull there so big a man could curl up inside it and sleep. That's honest, Joe, and I'll take you there sometime. A whole layer of shale, full of those bones.'

It was slow going. The flat slab rock afforded treacherous footing for a shod horse. Reflected heat blistered their faces. There was no water in the bottom, and the cattle, unused to thirst on the lush Squawhammer, were bawling. After four miles they turned off along another big draw, and in the distance lay the flat shine of water.

It was a brackish little pond of spring runoff held by a dirt dam. Situated on higher ground were some sheds, a shanty, and a corral.

'This Art Gamey's?' Joe asked.

'Still looking for that appaloosa? Art's place is a hell of a lot harder to find than this.'

While the steers were drinking, knee-deep in muck and water, Joe followed Holly toward the cabin. Three dogs that looked like shepherds crossed with timber wolves came out to bark at them but cringed with tails wagging when Holly called them by name. Nobody was in sight, though the door to the shack was open. A gotch-eared bronc watched them over the top pole of the corral. They rode past a cache house built eight or ten feet above the ground on stilts covered by flattened-out tin cans to turn back the claws of marauding skunks and bobcats. Meat had been hung in strips to dry along the sunny side while countless flies swarmed around it.

'He's around someplace. Wouldn't leave those dogs here while he was jerking meat.'

Holly stopped by a shed hung with clusters of rusty traps and let his eyes sweep the hillside. An old man came in sight with a gun across his arm and started down, splay-footed in his moccasins.

Holly shouted, 'Hello, Pete!' and said to Joe: 'That's old Pete Fontaine. You know him, don't you?'

Pete was a French-breed, a wolfer who'd lived in the breaks ever since Joe could remember. He used to stop at the ranch on his way to Box Elder, but that had been years ago.

'You got heem plenty steer thees tam,' Pete said in his nasal coyote-French accent. 'What brand is thees? D bar H? You rustle all them damn' steer in one day?'

He was grinning, showing his brownish teeth. Holly didn't bother to explain to him. He said: 'Sure, there's nothing chippy about us Wolvertons. Know my kid brother, Pete?'

'*Dieu!* I don' see heem in long tam.'

Pete leaned his rifle against a warped gold rocker. He was unspeakably dirty. He probably had not removed his shirt or trousers since they had been purchased, and now they were half worn out. Like most trappers, he used part of the summer to concoct lures from the musk glands and urine of wild animals, and it was bad to have him on the upwind side. He was below average in height, his legs were slightly bowed, and his body was too large for them, a characteristic he had inherited from his Assiniboin mother.

Holly said: 'Thought maybe you needed some fresh meat. Looks like hunting's been good, though.' He pointed to the jerky hanging stiff and brown by the cache house. 'What's that, buffalo?'

'Sure. Heem buffalo. White man buffalo. Five, six days ago I jump heem Snaky G steer.'

It was common knowledge that wolfers like Pete shot any stray they happened to run across in the badlands.

'Could you use another one?'

'Sure.'

Holly had already drawn his rifle from the scabbard. Before Joe realized what he was about, he tossed it to his shoulder, beaded, and fired. The brindle steer had waded from the mud and was facing them. The bullet knocked him to his knees, and he slowly rolled over and died. 'There's another one for you. Divide it up with old Packy and tell him where it came from.'

'Sure.' Pete didn't ask any questions. He was too glad to get the meat.

Holly walked down to the shadow of the cache house, talking to Pete. He accepted some strips of jerky which had attained the consistency of sole leather but said No to Pete's suggestion that he cook dinner. Joe, in the meantime, swapped horses, so there was no delay in getting the steers in movement again.

'Hungry?' Holly asked. He knew how Joe had been sickened by the thought of eating the wolfer's cooking. 'Want to go back and have a bowl of Pete's mulligan?'

82

'I'd die first.'

'The hell you would! You get hungry enough and Pete's grub would taste like something out of a Northern Pacific dining car. Did I ever tell you about the stew I ate in an Arapaho lodge down on the Big Horn?'

While they rode up the dusty hot bottoms, Holly told his story.

'It was December, couple years ago, and I was headed up from the Wind River with the weather cold as a banker's handshake. I'd figured on crossing to Coyote Wells for the coach, but the stage road was snowed full, and I knew my bronc would never make it crossing drifts, so I kept heading north, following the ridge where the snow was blowed off. This story ain't making you too cold, is it?'

'I'll live.'

'Well, I ran out of grub, and I was two days with nothing but a jackrabbit, heading for a trapper's cabin I knew about, but when I got there it was snowed over and nobody had broke in all year. I knew I'd made a mistake in not heading for the Wells, drifts or no, but it was too late then, so I kept on traveling north with it forty below and me three days without food. I was so lank you could have counted the joints in my backbone from the belly side. I figured it was about up with me when I hove over the ridge at the mouth of the Paint, and there was a village of Arapahos. Just hide teepees and wickiups, fifty or sixty of 'em, but to me it looked big as Denver. It happened I'd met a couple of the chiefs when I was delivering government beef the summer before, and they entertained me like I was Grover Cleveland. Squaws cooked me up a big stew with camas roots and dried choke-cherries and meat. Plenty of meat. Never did ask just what kind of animal the meat came off from, but I'll say this: he was bigger than a jackrabbit and a lot smaller than a deer. It was rare, and when you tried to chew it, it was tough, but it sure did feel good going down.'

Joe said, 'Maybe it was mutton.'

'I'd rather eat dog.'

They found a spring and camped by it. Joe was still thinking about getting so hungry you'd eat dog. He said, 'If I was up against it, I'd rather eat horse than dog.'

'That's because you're not smart as an Injun. When an Injun gets to eating his own camp up, he'll take the dogs first because he can get along without 'em. He needs his horse to ride on if he expects to get game.'

'Those Gros Ventres up at Sky Butte ate their horses one year. That's what Hap claimed.'

'The Cheyennes on Tongue River cooked and ate their hide teepees. I'd hate to of died in that camp. They'd never have found enough of you for a Christian burial.'

'Injuns do that?'

'No, I guess they don't. I heard of a white

man turning cannibal, but not an Injun.'

Joe knew that Holly liked the Indians. There were some folks around Box Elder who claimed the Wolvertons had Indian blood, but old Clay said it was a dirty lie.

'Why you like Injuns, Holly?'

'I don't know. I guess it's because they're always getting kicked around.'

The following noon found them in a hidden valley, green with grass and cottonwoods. There they left the herd and started the long climb to a ridge crest.

'Lost?' Holly asked.

'I'd find my way out.'

'Sure you would, only you might run into some tough miles.' He pointed out a sharp-backed ridge. 'If you're ever down here alone, looking for a way out, that one will take you almost to the line shack. Turn the other way, and you'll be close to Art Gamey's. I wouldn't advise going to Art's by yourself, though.'

'Should think you'd be worried, leaving the stock here.'

'On account of Art? He might knock one down for meat, but he won't bother the herd. Art's all right.'

'I ain't seen my appaloosa back.'

'Let's go down there now. If Art's around we'll be able to collect that Injun pony or a better one. I'll bet my hat on it.'

An hour's ride placed them in another of the ancient river valleys shaded by cottonwoods. Horse trails ran everywhere. They crossed the twin ruts of a wagon road which evidently led down to the river. The valley narrowed between walls of sandrock. Holly said, 'Never ride in without giving them warning,' and fired his six-shooter into the air.

They waited for five minutes after the shot's echo died away. Then somebody shouted down from the rocks. 'Holly?'

'Yes.'

'It's all right.'

They rode through the narrows. A shiftless-looking old man was walking back around the hill trail with a rifle in the crook of his arm. The valley broadened to a quarter-mile in width. A creek no wider than a man's two palms flowed between shelving banks, hidden by rose thorns. Against a bare rise of hillside stood some horse corrals, sheds, and cabins. After all Joe had heard about Gamey's place, it didn't look like much.

Five men were loafing in the shade of the blacksmith shop. Excepting one who was an Indian, they looked like ordinary punchers, but Joe knew they were rustlers involved in Gamey's business of scattering stolen horses across half the Northwest.

'That your kid brother?' one of them asked Holly. He was a rusty-complexioned man of about thirty. He kept picking at his teeth with a spear of grass, looking at Joe. 'Last time I recall, you were inside that line shanty on

Whiterock Crick, just more'n making your old Henry gun talk.'

Joe had an idea that he had seen him somewhere a long time before that. He couldn't place him until Holly said, 'You remember Muddy, don't you?' and he knew it was Muddy McBride, brother of Jerry McBride, the rustler North had killed that day on the roundup. Perhaps he'd never seen Muddy before. It was just that he recalled the dying face of his brother so well.

Holly asked, 'Art around?'

'Not for a week. Might be in Dakota by this time.'

'Might be in hell,' a heavy-shouldered man said, and they all laughed.

'We were looking for Joe's appaloosa. Art promised to bring him back.'

They looked blank at mention of the appaloosa. Then Muddy remembered and said, 'Oh, that horse Red got at your corral.'

The Indian said: 'I didn' see that appaloosy in three week. I think he's in with that herd Red drive down to Bitterroot.'

Muddy said: 'Whyn't you see Art about it? He probably forgot. Should have been here last week and maybe you could have talked him out of one of them Kentucky five-gaiters he picked up across the river from Terry. My Gawd, those were *horses*.'

When they rode up-valley, Joe said, 'I'll never see that appaloosa again, or not even as much as a gotch-eared bronc. Damn' horse rustler!'

'Art'll fix you up. He's not so bad. Come down here with the sheriff on your tail and Art'd grubstake you for a year.'

The valley kept narrowing and widening. After three or four miles, Holly turned up a coulee that looked like twenty other coulees, saying: 'Try and remember this one. See that rock? Looks like a toadstool. That's how I always tell.'

The coulee deepened and steepened, cutting the northward-trending ridges. After a few miles it came to its apparent termination in a tumble of sandrock boulders beneath towering cliffs. There Holly dismounted, saying, 'We'll be on foot a ways,' and led his horse up a tortuous switchback.

A ten-minute climb took them over a hump of slide rock. There, from a new angle, what had looked like solid cliff was gashed deeply by erosion. At one time the gash had probably gone completely through the ridge, but rock had fallen, half filling it.

The rough trail continued, and Holly followed it. Never was more than forty or fifty feet of it visible ahead of them, but at each apparent termination it opened again, until at last, between rock pile and cliff, it dropped into a cavernlike slot beneath an undercut strata of quartzite.

There Holly's horse balked and had to be

blindfolded, but once he was led inside the others followed. The floor was uneven but deeply padded with dirt and the litter of coyotes and mountain lions that had denned there for centuries. The roof kept pitching down above them, until at times there was scant clearance for the packsaddles. Here and there a shaft of sunshine found its way through a crevice in the over-lying rock, so that in no place in its fifty yards of length was it dark. They emerged on the other side of the ridge and started downhill among cliffs and pillars overlooking another big, barren valley.

Descending, climbing again, always returning to a course east of south, they reached the prairie rim. They were at Wing Coulee, only a short ride from the home ranch.

Days in a country strange to him had driven the thought of Alvis Brewer from Joe's mind. Now he thought of him and said: 'Think you dare show up? North'll have the Association on the prod for sure after that shooting.'

'I just outdrew Brewer. It's happened before. No shortage of gunhawks. North'll replace him. Losing Brewer will worry him less than losing a steer.'

The house was dark and Ma was in bed when they got there. She got up, so relieved she almost cried. She did not mention the shooting, but Joe knew she had heard and had been at home worrying for fear North and his gunmen had trailed them and killed them.

She shook down the fire, made coffee, a johnnycake, and a thick, syrupy raisin pie. When Joe awoke, it was hot morning, and he could hear Ma and Holly arguing outside. He got up and stood by the open window. They were on the other side of the house and she was saying: 'What you want to stay here for? Whyn't you take Joe and head for Milk River? Jim Hill's extending his line through that country. There's a real chance for a couple of boys with gumption.'

'Ma, if you don't want me working for you any more—'

'It ain't that. You know it ain't. It's this killing. One killing never settled anything. I been in this country long enough to see things shape up and know what always comes of it. Big outfits spreading out and little fellows trying to squeeze in. We're headed toward a blow-up, a real first-class range war, with you and that kid in there right in the middle of it. If you have no consideration of me or yourself, you ought to have some for Joe.'

It angered Joe to think she was making a child of him.

Holly hadn't said anything, so Ma went on: 'Oh, I know why you won't leave. Its on account of that Eaton girl. Poor little thing. What do you plan to do about her? Marry her? What you got to give her?'

'Was she here looking for me again?'

'Yes, she was here looking for you! One of

these days her daddy will follow her, and when he does—'

'Stop it, Ma. When was she here?'

Joe couldn't hear what Ma said, but he had that unpleasant, angry sensation again, that feeling of hot and cold. He turned away from the window and started pulling his levis on. He wondered what was wrong with himself. Was it that he liked Holly so well he didn't want any girl coming ahead of himself?

Next day, when he came back from a ride up Gros Ventre Creek, he saw two horses tied to the awning posts. They carried the Grant County brand, so it was no surprise to hear Dad Tripp inside talking to Ma.

Dad Tripp was a tall man, lean and slightly bent in the shoulders, with a gray mustache, the underside of which had turned brown from cigarette smoke. He had been sheriff of Grant County ever since it was carved from Dawson in 1882. Standing at one side was Wasey Stager.

Dad spun around at the sound of Joe's boot heels, expecting Holly. He said, 'Hello, Joe. Your brother around?'

'What do you care if he's around?'

Tripp's face went rigid with anger at Joe's tone. He restrained an impulse and said: 'That's no way to talk to me. If you think I got elected sheriff of Grant County to let slick kids hand me their lip, you better realign your sights. Now, I asked where he was and I want a decent answer.'

Joe had always liked Dad Tripp, and now he wished he hadn't spoken quite as he had. Still, he didn't back water. He faced Dad with his jaw out and said: 'I asked why you cared if he was around. What's wrong with that?'

'Sometimes it's not what a man says but the way he says it. You know why I want him. I want him on account of that shooting on Squawhammer, and I want you, too, for witness.'

'So the Association's raising hell about that tough Wyoming gunman they brought in!'

'Association's got the same rights as anybody else.'

'They rode down and shot our Coalbank line shack full of holes, killed a man in the corral, and tried to kill me, but I didn't notice the Sheriff's office bustin' its britches that time.'

Dad was still angry, but Joe was on better ground now and he didn't care. He was going to say a whole lot more but Ma got between them.

She said to Dad: 'It's true! You don't bust your britches for us. That's why you're getting red in the neck, because it is true.'

Dad took a deep breath. 'Ma, we been friends for going on ten year—'

'Don't talk about friendship to me. My boys ride yonder to the Squawhammer and try to gather their own stock like the Association ordered them, and when a bunch of hired, brought-in gunmen start a ruckus, who do you come around arresting?'

'Ma, that talk don't add up. What do you expect me to do, arrest a dead man?'

'My boy shot in self-defense.'

'Then he'll be turned free.'

'North and that polished mule thief Major Eaton have a deadfall fixed or they wouldn't send you here.'

'I'm not going to argue any more. Its for Holly's good if he lets me take him in. It's for the good of everybody concerned. You tell me where he is.'

'I'll tell you nothing. Get out of my house.'

'All right, Ma, if that's the way you want it.'

Slager had stayed back, against one wall, where he could keep the whole room under his gaze. When he did not immediately start with Dad toward the door, she turned on him, 'And you get out, too!' He started to say something, but she bellowed him down. 'Don't open your trap at me, you two-bit flunkey. That's what you are—a two-bit flunkey for the Association!'

Dad said, 'Come on, Slag.' He drew up with his tall form framed in the door, and Joe knew someone was coming. It was Holly, walking at his easy amble up from the corral.

'Hello, Dad,' Holly said. 'You looking for me on account of Brewer?'

Dad laughed and said in a relieved voice:

'I'm glad somebody's got sense around here. Yeah, Holly, I'm looking for you on account of Brewer. I got a warrant. I got to take you in.'

'Mind if I pack my war bag?'

'Go ahead.'

Dad sat on the bench outside and smoked, the cigarette drooping beneath his mustache. Joe followed Holly inside the bedroom and watched while he went through the drawers of a battered old bureau, getting out his town clothes that had been stored there for months.

Joe asked, 'Why you letting him take you in? They got some sort of a deadfall fixed up—'

'Can't you see I either got to go in with him or get clear out of the country? If I just try to lay low, I'm a fugitive wanted for murder and legal game for the first Association gunman that can get his sights on me.'

'And this way they'll hang you!'

'I don't think so. I've seen plenty of men arrested for gun-fight killings, but I never saw any convictions.'

CHAPTER SEVEN

It was a quiet night in Box Elder. Joe came from the sheriff's office and paused a moment, wondering what he ought to do. Then he heard Dad Tripp speak his name and come outside after him.

Dad laid a hand on his shoulder and said: 'You can get him out on bail, I suppose, if you want to try for it, but it'll only be three weeks before Judge Rakestraw comes. I'd leave him in if I was you.'

He knew that Dad had come outside so Slager wouldn't hear him. 'You mean North's gunmen might try to kill him?'

'No, I didn't mean that. Not exactly. Only thing is, if he's inside it'll keep him out of arguments. Brewer has friends. You know how these things are.'

'Yeah, I know.'

'You'll explain it to Ma?'

'I'll tell her what you said.'

He slapped Joe on the shoulder in parting. 'No hard feelings about this morning?'

'Of course not.'

'Staying in town tonight?' Dad called from the jail door. 'You can bed down in here if you'd like.'

Holly had given him a $20 gold piece, telling him to go first class, so he said, 'Thanks, but I'll put up at the Stockman's Hotel.'

Only once before had Joe ever gone to bed between sheets. He couldn't sleep for hours. When he awoke, the sun coming through the window told him it was late. Strange voices and the jingle of harness chains drifted from the street under his window. He got up and looked out.

A jerkline mule outfit maneuvered around to the Barker Company's side platform and commenced unloading flour. Directly across was the barbershop. He could look in the front window and see a man in the chair and another, with a fresh haircut and shave, putting his collar and tie back on. He scrutinized himself in the rusty mirror. His hair hung over the back of his shirt collar and there was a quarter-inch of whiskers on his chin. He felt out of place in town, anyway, and conscious of his shaggy appearance. Though he dreaded going downstairs through the hotel lobby, he did so, crossed to the barbershop, and came out an hour later, shaved, and with a cream-white strip around his ears and the back of his neck where the long hair had been clipped away.

He had started across the dusty street, trying to get his hat placed so that it didn't feel too big for his head, when he saw Ned Garfield, Dick Dean, and a third man come from the Elkhorn Saloon.

With thumping heart he walked straight on, to Charley Hop's café. Later, at the jail, he said to Dad Tripp: 'North's gun wranglers are in town. They didn't wait long, did they?'

The usual cigarette hung under Dad's mustache. 'You see what I was talking about? If Holly was out he'd run into them, and something would be bound to happen. That Garfield's bad medicine.'

Joe slid back his hat, as he had seen Holly do, and said, 'Holly'd beat him to the draw and kill him.'

'He might and he might not. You flip a coin, and I'll give you the winner of that fight. Garfield's killed at least six men. Six they know about. He ain't the kind that tries to talk up a reputation.'

'Wonder North isn't here.'

'He's at Musselshell, I suppose.' Dad winked. 'He's got a girl over there. He's been riding over to see Ruby Tolliver.'

Joe surmised he should know who Ruby Tolliver was, so he laughed along with Dad.

Joe talked to Holly for half an hour, picked up some groceries Ma wanted, and with the sack roped to the back of his saddle, rode back to the ranch. He met Ma driving some cows and calves along the creek bottoms. She was dressed like a man; a stranger might have thought she was a man. She listened to what he had to say without putting in twenty words of her own during the hour it took them to reach the corrals.

He walked with her to the porch, where she stepped on the jack and started tugging off her old runover riding boots.

'He'll be all right, Ma.'

She growled, 'He should never have come home.'

'Well, what if he did go and hide out? It'd be open season on him and all legal. They'd get him the first time he showed his head out of the badlands.'

'He needn't stop at the badlands. He could clear all the way out of the country. He done it before.'

'Holly's not letting anybody *run* him out.'

'No, he's not letting anybody run *him* out. He'll stay. He'll stay right here and buck the percentages, and pretty soon the *percentages* will run out. Cray North's got things rigged in his favor, and he'll take just so much. If you want my opinion, we pushed North past his limit already.'

She walked inside, the slivery floor catching her stockinged feet. Joe followed and said: 'I wouldn't lay too much money against Holly. He's been around. He'll land on his feet.'

She gave him a long look, lifted the sack of provisions with one arm, and dumped it on the table. 'Oh, I get so sick of this fighting. All that man talk and false pride. I get so sick of waking up in the morning and wondering if I got anybody left,'

Ma would get in these moods sometimes, and she'd want to grab him and get him in her lap and cry over him. He was afraid of that now. He backed out of the door and went to get a pan of oats for his horse.

Hap Williams saw him and sneaked around through the horse shed so that he couldn't be seen from the house. 'Ps-s-st!' Hap whispered. 'Joe, can you hear me?'

'Yeah, I can hear you.' Hap was old and getting childish. Crazy from trying to find the long end of a square quilt, as the saying went. He'd been snowed up in too many line shacks for too many long winters.

'Chad Newhall and Stellingworth and a couple others was here after you left yesterday. Did Ma tell you?'

'No. What'd they want?'

'I'll tell you what they want!' Hap had his gun strapped on again, so Joe knew there'd been fight talk in the air. More and more of late years Hap had liked to talk gunfight, though he was harmless and had never shot at a man in his life. 'They were gunned up and looking for men. They're getting ready to blast the insides out of the Association if any more outside killers are brought in. They want the Winged W to join up with the other small outfits and form an association of their own.'

'How many they got?'

'I don't know. I couldn't hear everything they said. Don't let Ma know I told you. She said for 'em to keep away from you. She told 'em she wasn't going to have you shot in any range war.'

'Where'd they go?'

He motioned back toward the Thirty Mile. 'Yonder, I guess. I have an idea they'll try to line up them two-bit homesteaders from down toward Woodhawk Grove.'

After eating, Joe said he was going to check

on some steers at Wing Coulee, but once out of sight he turned northeast toward the Thirty Mile and followed the rims until he could see the bleached shanty and corrals where Chad Newhall and his big family lived. One lonely pinto bronc was switching flies in the corral, so he knew the men had gone elsewhere. He kept riding, eastward now, and that evening, from far away, he looked across rolling grass country at the Goosebill home ranch.

There were many acres of sheds and pole corrals, dominated by Major Eaton's house, which stood imposingly on rising ground, among cottonwoods. It was a two-story house, white-painted, with a porch that doubled its apparent size. Two other white houses were somewhat removed, on a bench overlooking Goosebill Creek. In one of these Alf Koenig, a bachelor, lived by himself; the other was a mess house for Koenig and some of the top hands. The cowboys' bunkhouses were at the lower ends of the corrals, nearly half a mile down the creek. It looked like headquarters for a big outfit, and it was—bigger than either the Great Western or the TN. He'd once heard Preacher Tom say it controlled a stretch of country bigger than Connecticut.

Joe had only the haziest idea of where Connecticut was. It was back East somewhere, in a country frequented by dudes. He'd heard a lot of bunkhouse talk about dudes. They were pallid men in serge suits and button shoes, with hard hats on their heads, a lily-livered lot. Almost any night, in a big bunkhouse like those on the Goosebill, or on the roundup lying around the chuckwagon fire, you could hear cowboys bragging in their soft Southwestern drawls about getting full of likker and cutting airholes through a dude's plug hat.

'It war in Miles four year ago,' he could remember Tige Mitchell saying, 'and I'd taken on such a load of strongwater that both my legs thought the other one had gone and joined the Confed'racy. Well, I came out of the Drover's Saloon, and there, standing in front of me, was this dude. I says, 'Glad to see you come to the dance.' 'What dance?' says he. 'This dance,' says I, and I cut loose. You can talk about your minstrel-show jigs; this dude laid it over anything I ever seen, and I been to Cheyenne and Denver both. I know it won't sound reasonable, but I cut the buttons right off his shoes, and when he hit the lower end of town he war barefooted . . .'

Joe had heard that Major Eaton wanted Ellen to be educated so that she would be good enough to marry some dude. He couldn't understand a man's feeling that way. It seemed like one woman marrying another, because to his mind a dude wasn't a man at all.

Someone was walking toward the big house. It was so far away he couldn't tell whether it was a man or a woman. He imagined it to be

Ellen. He tried to remember her face, the way it had been that night when he came upon her talking to Holly. Then once again that hot-and-cold feeling passed over him.

Without realizing it, he spurred his horse, and for a short time rode at a gallop northward. He slowed, kept at a steady, single-footing gait until the sun set, and at darkness he dropped down to the stage road and Goosebill Creek.

The Goosebill followed a broad valley, sparsely wooded. At one time Eaton had run cattle along the entire length of it, but now some of the best acres had been taken up under the Veterans' Act of 1872. Ten miles farther and the road would take him to Woodhawk Grove, with its steamboat landing and cable ferry.

He saw a lighted cabin window and rode toward it. The place, he thought, belonged to a man by the name of Bill Johns. He pulled up by some pole corrals. There were only two horses around; there was no sign of men or sound of voices from the cabin.

He heard movement and turned in the saddle, his right hand dropping automatically to the gun at his hip.

A woman said, 'Keep your hand away from that gun!' Her voice was loud and she was forcing it, but she failed to cover up an underlying shake of fear.

He said, 'I'm meaning no harm.'

'Who you got with you?'

'Nobody.' He tried to make her out, but she was deep in the moon shadow at one side of the shed. 'Ain't this where Bill Johns lives?'

'What you want him for?'

'Nothing. I just heard that Chad Newhall and some of the fellows were headed this way.'

'Who are you?'

'Joe Wolverton.'

A child wailed from inside the shanty: 'Who is it, Ma? Are you all right, Ma?' and started crying at the top of his voice.

She shouted: 'I'm all right. You stay where I put you!' She edged into the moonlight, the rifle in her hands still pointed. She was a bleached, worn-out-looking woman who might have been twenty-five or forty. She wore a dress that had been hand-sewn from flour sacking but, unlike Ma, she didn't look like the kind who should be dressed that way. There was nothing masculine about her. She had a stiffly erect look of one who kept herself going by nerve.

'Look out for the gun,' Joe said, noticing that her thumb was crooked around the hammer, partly cocking it.

She pointed the barrel down and said: 'What happened? What did they do to your brother?'

He knew then that Newhall and the others had been there and that her husband had gone on down the creek with them. 'He's in jail.

103

He'll be up for trial when Rakestraw comes three weeks from now.'

'Trial!' She tossed her head back with a laugh that had the unsteady note of a string drawn too tight. 'You can call it a trial if you want to! I think it'll be a legal lynching.'

The gun and the bitterness of her voice told him they'd been having trouble with the big outfits—probably with the Goosebill.

He asked, 'Eaton giving you a rough ride?'

'We had eighty acres of the finest oats you ever laid eyes on this summer. After two years of bad crops, we had it! Then Eaton's steers took it clean. Broke down the fence, and when they were through it looked like it had been plowed over again. Eaton—that dirty government mule thief!'

It was common talk that Eaton had resigned his commission in the cavalry under the threat of a court-martial for selling government stock and substituting bone-bag castoffs from the wagon trains. He wasn't the first one who got his start in the ranching business that way.

Joe said, 'See Eaton about the oats?'

'My man went up there, and Eaton wouldn't even talk to him. Alf Koenig did. Looked down his nose and said he'd take it up with the boss. Offered to buy us out. Eight hundred with $20 a head on our beef tally this fall. My man wanted to sell. I said No, I'd sit in a dugout and eat turnips before I sold to him.'

Joe wanted to go, but she got hold of the

loose end of his latigo strap and followed, still talking.

'You Wolvertons got the right idea. Gun them down when they get tough. Just get tougher than they are. That's what I told those fellows when they came for my man tonight.'

'Where were they headed from here?'

'To Horseshoe Conners's, I guess.'

She had to drop the latigo or wade the creek. He waved to her and cut back to the stage road. In another hour and a half he caught sight of Conners's cabin, about a mile up-valley from the Missouri.

A lamp was burning inside, and he could see the shadow movements of men. Chad Newhall heard the jingle of his spurs as he walked up from the corral. He peered outside and said, 'Joe?'

'Yeah.'

'Its Joe Wolverton,' Chad said to those inside. Joe was aware of their mutter of response. It felt good to be somebody. With Holly in jail, he was top man in the Wolverton outfit.

He stopped in the door to look around. After the long darkness the kerosene lamp seemed very bright. Men sat on benches, and when benches ran out, on the floor. There were fourteen, and he knew about half of them. For the most part they were homesteaders, Union Army veterans, men who'd passed the forty mark and were beginning to lose their taste for cowboying and who wanted a place of their own. It surprised him to see that Muddy McBride was there. He'd never thought of McBride as being anything but a rustler, hiding out in the badlands.

'You here?' He didn't intend it to sound the way it did. The words just slipped out.

'Why shouldn't I be?' McBride asked with an edge on his voice. 'Us McBrides been kicked around for a long time. We even been kicked around by the Wolvertons when they was riding high, but I hold no grudges. I got as much score to settle as anybody. Maybe you forgot, but Cray North was the man that killed my brother.'

'I didn't mean anything. I just thought you were—' He stopped, not wanting to mention Art Gamey's. 'I thought you were away yonder.'

McBride could see that the others were curious, so he laughed and said: 'Joe and me was in church together three, four days ago. Little old church in the wildwood.'

Newhall said to Joe, 'What'd they do about Holly?'

'He's locked up. We didn't ask for bail. He'll be charged when Judge Rakestraw comes. That'll be three weeks.'

McBride said: 'Holly must have been eating locoweed to give himself up like that. Judge Rakestraw'll hang him.' From one side of his mouth, while lighting a cigarette, he called Rakestraw a string of vile names. 'He's looking to be elected governor. Playing up to the big interests. He'll hop when the Association snaps the whip.'

Newhall said: 'Rakestraw'll do nothing that will cost him votes. Thing for us to do is ride in when the time comes and let him see how the cards lie. It'll show that damned Association how they lie, too.'

Bill Johns, a powerful but weak-jawed man, said, 'How many professional gunmen they got now?'

Joe said, 'North has ten or twelve.'

McBride cut in again. 'They keep bringing 'em in all the time. I understand Limpy Travis is riding for the Goosebill now. He was one of the big guns in the Pease-Henshaw war. For all we know, Nenus and Simmons have hired some guns, too. I'll lay money the Association has twenty professionals on its payroll, and that doesn't count in the cowboys who'd like to cut themselves a cold-meat notch at our expense. They're getting fixed to clean us out unless we start cleaning them first. I'm not in favor of waiting for Rakestraw to come. Let's us go for them. I know a spot on that Coalbank road where twelve rifles could sure as hell cut North down to size.'

Somebody said, 'I'll have no part of bushwhack.'

'I knew you wouldn't. Turn the other cheek.

Wait till they burn you out. If you're lucky, maybe they won't fit you with a lariat cravat. Maybe they'll just let you get out of the country. That's the old hoe-man spirit.'

Newhall said: 'All the Association aren't hotheaded like North. Nenus and Eaton will pull back if they see we're ready to battle. And the place to show 'em is in town, when they bring Holly up for trial. If we're there with sixty, seventy men, we'll throw the fear of hell into the judge, and maybe into those gunmen, too.'

'Where'll we find seventy men?' Conners asked.

'Clint Saxon is getting the small outfits from south of the TN range. He says the Dumas boys are on the prod, and that's eight right there. Maybe we won't have seventy, but I'll bet it'll be more than fifty.'

Johns whined: 'Somebody'll get drunk and somebody'll get shot. That's how those things always go.'

Muddy McBride said, 'Maybe you better stay home with your old woman.'

'I'll be there. I'll be there just like the rest of you.'

CHAPTER EIGHT

Judge Theodore Case Rakestraw arrived in Box Elder on July 25, a full eight days before his term of court was scheduled to commence. That he arrived early, without warning, was no accident. Judge Rakestraw had decided to attend the Midwestern Assembly of Republican Governors, Legislators, and Planners being held that year in Chicago, and keynoted by the great Robert Ingersoll. To be on hand for the first meeting on September 2, Judge Rakestraw found it necessary to lop a week off his Grant and his Dawson county terms of court. By arriving unexpectedly and immediately calling some of the civil suits before the interested parties had a chance to conquer the distances of the country and appear, he'd be able to set them over to the winter term. Judge Rakestraw had already built up an imposing calendar of such postponed cases by similar maneuvering in the past, but that did not greatly bother him. If his plans went right, he would shortly become governor and pass the calendar on to some helpless successor.

He spent his first two days in Box Elder getting the calendar in order, and on the third was ready for his criminal cases, chief of which pitted the Territory of Montana against Hollis

Wolverton, the charge—murder.

That morning, nearer midnight than dawn, Joe hitched the team to the buckboard and drove around to the house for Ma. She came out dressed in a black silk dress, wearing high-heeled button shoes that kept turning under her feet. It was a year since he had seen Ma dressed in anything except shirt and overalls.

When they were jouncing off, along the creek road, she asked, 'You've been seeing Conners and Newhall almost every night lately, haven't you?'

'Yeah.'

'What they got planned? Joe, I know something's going on. If Newhall thinks he can bullyrag that Judge—'

'They just want to see Holly don't get dealt to off'n a cold deck, that's all. It's nothing to get mad about.'

She jolted for a while and said, 'I'm not mad about it.' Her voice had an unusual gentleness when she went on, 'Don't you see, Joe? All I want is for you boys to come out all right. If this thing starts a range war, you'll be caught in the middle of it. Oh, I know how hard it is for kids to understand how an old woman feels.'

It was midafternoon when they got to town. The hitch racks were lined with saddle horses, and at least twenty rigs were scattered around the knoll beyond the Apex Stable. Men moved along the sidewalks or stood in groups talking quietly. It was not easy to tell one side from the other, because most of the men who had taken land under the Act had been punching cows themselves a couple of years before. There did not seem to be much drinking.

As he drove down the street, Joe could feel the eyes of people who turned to watch them. He guided the team across the gravel path and beneath the cottonwoods to the Stockman's Hotel.

Short gray-haired Ned Clayburn opened the door and said: 'I been saving a room for you, Mrs. Wolverton. I knew you'd be in.'

It surprised Ma that anybody would be that kind. She stopped and looked in his face, saying: 'Thank you, Mr. Clayburn. I'm sure that was thoughtful of you.'

Ma went to the room, washed, and brushed dust off her black silk dress. Dad Tripp was waiting in a lobby chair when she came down.

'I saw you drive in,' he said. 'I was about ready to go out after you. I didn't want you to think we were trying to pull a bottom card in calling the case early.'

'When does it start—the trial?'

'Well, he was in front of the judge this morning, but the case won't be called until tomorrow. You want to see him now?'

They found Holly in the largest of the four jail cells, lying on his back, reading a two-day-old copy of the Miles City *Daily Press.*

He looked at Ma's black dress and said: 'Ma, they'll see you in that get-up and think

111

you came for a hanging. Why'nt you wear the yellow dress I brought you from Miles City?'

'What would I be doing dressed in yellow with my boy up for murder?'

'Well, don't worry about it. I hear there's a dude putting on a magic-lantern show in the hall tonight. Joe, you take her over there and see that she has a good time.' He drew a $20 gold piece from his pocket and spun it high for Joe to catch. 'Here—blow that in!'

She said, 'Where you get that kind of money?'

'I got a sluice down in the coulee. Take it and paint the town.'

'Holly, this is nothing to joke about. You know all the trouble that's afoot? Chad Newhall and Stellingworth have been stirring up the small outfits for the last two weeks, and now they got 'em in here gunned up like Grant at Vicksburg.'

'Yeah. I know.' He was no longer smiling. He sat on the bunk, puffing his cigarette and looking out through the grated door. 'Well, what do you want me to do—plead guilty?'

'If you did and got off with a year or so, everything would blow over, and—'

Joe said, 'He ain't going to plead guilty!'

She motioned him to be quiet and kept talking, pleading with Holly. 'Don't you understand? The Association can't have their hand called and back down. They know they made a mistake in bringing charges. They thought you'd just clear out of the country when you heard the sheriff had a warrant. Then, when you gave yourself up, they had to go through with it. Sure, they picked a bad issue—Brewer so mean even his own friends didn't like him—but they're in it now and they'll carry through. They'll try to get a conviction and hang you or bury you in the pen for twenty years. If they can't, they'll get rough to save face. They'll gun you down when you try to leave the jail.'

'With Rakestraw looking on?'

'Yes, with him looking on!'

'Ma,' Holly said gently, 'I think you ought to go home.'

'You trying to tell me that—'

'I think it'd be better all around if you went home. Didn't you notice all those little two-bit ranchers out there, come in to make an issue of it? I didn't figure on being a hero and leading 'em against the Association, but now that they took it up I'm not running out.'

'I suppose it'll be a favor to them—getting them in a range war!'

'It'll come sooner or later.'

'You're stubborn! Worse'n your dad for being stubborn.'

'Ma, when I walk out of that courthouse I'll have my gun on. If I ride out of town without drawing a shot, I want everybody to know the reason. I don't want the Association saying they were too kindhearted to shoot a man in front of his ma.'

The town kept filling up. Dad Tripp deputized five men who patrolled the streets, ready to check the first flare of trouble. The bars were doing a good business, but scarcely anyone raised his voice; and when two young punchers from the TN started whooping and chap-fighting in the Shamrock, you could hear them down the street.

Heat of afternoon settled. A division in the crowd was now visible, with small ranchers headquartered at the Apex and men from the big outfits near the Stockman's Hotel.

About four o'clock, with Dad Tripp and his men breathing more easily, the Dumas boys rode into Main Street at a wary wolf trot, their broncs kicking a fine gumbo dust that hung yellowish in the late sun. There were eight of them, a gaunt, ragged-looking crew, announcing their readiness for trouble with Winchesters unsheathed, held across the pommels of their saddles. Dad Tripp saw them, walked to the middle of the street, stood with his hand on his hips, just above the butts of two guns, waiting.

Steve Dumas, about forty and the eldest of the brothers, was in the lead. He came straight toward Dad as though to ride him down, but Dad didn't move and Steve wheeled his horse around at the last instant.

Dad said: 'Steve, put your rifles back in the leather. We ain't had any trouble yet and you aren't starting it.'

Steve kept the gun as it was, his right hand through the lever, its barrel pinched between his waist and the saddle horn. There were streaks of tobacco juice down the corners of his mouth, painting an extra malevolence on his face. He said, 'Where's Tom Nenus?'

The Dumas boys had taken out claims along the water of the TN south range, and for a year they had carried on a long-range sniping with Nenus's men.

Dad said: 'I don't know where he is. He's behaving himself and everybody else is behaving himself. I got deputies scattered around town. I gave them orders to drop the first man that starts trouble. You've had your fair warning; now put up your guns.'

Steve sat with his legs ramrodded down in the stirrups as he swung around, while his eyes roved the sidewalks and the roofs on both sides. He spat and with a slouch of his long body bent and rammed the rifle back in its scabbard. Reluctantly, one after another, his brothers followed suit. When the last gun was out of sight, Dad turned and walked back toward the jail.

The Dumas boys continued their ride to the Apex corral without incident, and the crowd that had appeared so suddenly began to break away.

Joe had watched from the Barker Company platform. He crossed to the hotel and entered the lobby. Creighton North was standing near the barroom archway, talking to Tip Carslyle and a short, red-faced man whose name Joe didn't know.

It was the first time he'd seen North since that day at the line shack, and despite all the thinking and resolving he'd done, nothing had changed. He felt clammy and hollow. He walked with no sensation of walking. His instinct was to get out of sight, to pretend not to see him. Instead, with an effort, he looked straight into North's face. North's expression was stony, his eyes staring through him and beyond him, as though he didn't exist, and all the while he nodded at what Tip Carslyle had to say.

Short of breath and sweating, Joe climbed the stairs. In the dim hall he stopped and named North every vicious word he had at his command. It made him feel better. He opened the door to Ma's room and went inside.

She was sitting in a straight chair, staring out on the street with a flat lack of expression. Without glancing up she said: 'See the type you'll be fighting alongside of? The Dumases! Next we'll have to side with Gamey and McBride. See how far we're going for our friends? Pa would be out with a hang-rope for their kind.'

'They're just as good as that gunman bunch of North's!'

He sat with her for almost an hour. It was so

quiet he could hear the thud and jingle of men along the walks. At last, with the sun gone beyond the buildings, he said, 'Want to eat?'

'You go ahead, Joe. I ain't hungry.'

'But you haven't had a thing since before daylight.'

'I couldn't swallow. It'd stick in my throat.'

'Ma, you shouldn't get so upset. I'll bet nothing happens. Not tonight, anyhow. Let's eat and go to that lantern show like Holly told us.'

'You think I could set and watch a show with a two-to-one bet hanging over me that my own child will lay dead in that street before this time tomorrow? And I don't want you going, either.'

He sat, like her, staring at the street. He didn't know what to say to Ma. Sometimes she seemed to be another person. At last he rose and went to the door. 'Sure you don't want something?'

'You can bring me a pot of tea.'

He had to wait his turn at the Chinese café. He came back, bringing Ma a ham sandwich as well as the tea. He was placing them before her, on the windowsill, when someone rapped at the door. It was a light tap. He opened the door and saw Ellen Eaton.

She looked thin and pretty and scared. She seemed to be smaller than the last time he had seen her. It was the clothes she wore—a dark brown blouse and divided skirt instead of

117

starched linen and lace that puffed away from her slim body.

She stood staring at Joe. Her lips were parted, and the rapid rise and fall of her breast showed her excitement.

Ma squeaked around in her chair to see who it was. 'Come in, child,' she said.

Ellen said, 'All right,' and stepped inside. She closed the door and leaned back against it.

Ma said: 'Child, you're sure it's all right for you to come here? Your daddy's in town, isn't he?'

'Yes, but he didn't see me. I didn't come through the lobby.'

'He knows you're in town, though. He'll—'

'He thinks I'm at the ranch.'

Joe said, 'What d' we care about him?'

'You care if Ellen gets in trouble, don't you?'

Ellen crossed in front of him and seated herself on the edge of the bed, looking rigid and uncomfortable. She had come close to Joe, leaving a stir of air with the clean perfume of her body on it. It seemed almost like touching her.

Ma said: 'Girl, aren't you taking an awful chance? What if he found out you was seeing us. You know how he is.'

'I don't care!' she said fiercely, as though she hated him, and Joe stared at her. He had never imagined her capable of feeling that way toward anyone.

Ma said: 'Yes, you do. He's your daddy, and you care whether you know it now or not. Blood's thicker'n water. Anyhow, he's right.'

'He's not right!'

'He's right about Holly.' Ma checked her voice and went on. 'I don't blame him for driving Holly away. What if you did get married? Holly ain't got anything but the clothes on his back. He never will have. What could he ever offer you? Some dirt-floored shack in a coulee, and you watching the skyline every day wondering if he'd come home roped over the back of his horse.'

'He'd be all right if they just gave him a chance.' She didn't sound as though she really believed it herself.

'He had a chance. I told him and Joe to trail what stock we got to that new Injun land they threw open on Milk River. Neither of 'em would even give thought to it. They gave me a lot of man talk about not being run off the range by North and the Association.'

Joe noticed that Ellen's hands were clenched together so hard that her knuckles looked like ivory.

She said: 'Ma, that's what I'm scared about-the Association. I heard Dad and Alf Koenig talking last night at the ranch. They're bringing men in. All the big outfits are. They had a messenger riding from one ranch to the other, telling them all to come in. They think Rakestraw will turn him loose; I heard that

119

much. I'm scared, Ma. I'm scared they'll try to grab him when he comes out of the jail.'

'I tried to tell him that. He won't listen to me; maybe he will to you. No, wait! I don't want you going to see him. You shouldn't have come at all.'

Joe said, 'We got a few guns on our side, too, in case you didn't notice.'

Ellen whispered: 'They'll kill him! They might not even wait till tomorrow.'

Ma took one bite of the sandwich, managed to swallow it, and put the rest aside. She got up and said, 'Maybe there's still something I can do.'

Joe didn't realize she was leaving until her hand was on the knob. He cried, 'What are you going to do?'

'I'm going to see Creighton North.'

'What for?'

'What d' you think for?' She went outside. Joe grabbed the knob. She swung her body powerfully and jerked it from his fingers. It surprised him, and during his moment of hesitation Ellen got in front of him.

Ellen said, 'Joe, let her do what she wants to.'

'I'm not letting her beg anything from North.'

He tried to push her out of the way. She had a wiry, unexpected strength. He got her aside, but she clutched his arm with both hands.

She was whispering, breathing from effort:

'Joe, stay here! North hates you. He'd kill you, Joe. Dad says he'll kill you some time.'

Her words seemed to assume he'd be no match for North. It made him furious. It seemed to him that she knew how he felt, how yellow he was. She was still holding him, hanging with all her weight on his arm. He pivoted and flung her away, harder than he intended. Her shoulder struck the door casing and she fell to her knees. Her hat was off, her hair loose and across her face.

Joe clutched his gun, half drew it. She was still there and wouldn't get out of his way.

'I'll kill him,' he said, almost sobbing. 'I'll show you I'm not scared of him. I'll hunt him down and kill him.'

For a few seconds he'd almost convinced himself, he thought he *did* have the kind of nerve that would let him walk up to North, call him what he was, and shoot it out.

He started around her toward the door, but she grabbed him again, just as he had expected her to do. He could have got loose but he used only half his strength. He let her pull him away to mid-room. He couldn't go through with it and face North.

She said, 'Joe, let me have your gun.'

She got it in both hands and backed away. She looked around, not knowing what to do with it, then let it fall and kicked it under the bed.

She said: 'You're worse than Holly. Don't

you know he has a gang of hired gunmen at his back?'

It made him feel better when she put it that way. He sat down on the bed and held his head in his hands. He was winded. He noticed that the back of his hand was scratched and bleeding.

She stood over him. He could sense the nearness of her body. 'Joe. Joe, I'm sorry.'

He thought she was talking about the cut. 'It's nothing.'

'He wouldn't shoot it out with you. He's not that kind. No matter where he goes, Garfield or Tripplett are with him, especially now, when he's expecting somebody to gun for him. You wouldn't have a chance.'

She sat down beside him. Having her so close made him feel unsteady. He didn't look at her. He didn't dare. He stared at his hand, at the blood coming from it. Her shoulder touched him. She was moving, hunting for something. She drew a tiny balled-up handkerchief from her blouse, shook it out, and pressed it tightly to the back of his hand.

They sat without moving or speaking for a long time, while the last twilight faded and a night breeze stirred the curtains. The tension of the day seemed to have relaxed, and they could hear the sound of voices and laughter. Far away, someone played a piano. It came through the window with a minute clarity, the 'Blue Velvet Waltz,' played in ragtime.

At last Joe forced himself to say, 'You like Holly, don't you?'

She whispered, 'Yes.'

He wanted her to like Holly. He tried to tell himself that, but he knew it was a lie. His cheeks felt hot. He was glad the room was dark, too dark for her to see.

CHAPTER NINE

After closing the door, Ma waited for a while to see if Joe would try to follow her; when he didn't, she walked downstairs to the lobby. No one was there except old Dave Kellets, decked out in his army coat with its Mexican campaign ribbon. Everyone seemed to be in the bar. She walked as far as the arch. In a moment Tom Nenus noticed her, put down his watered whisky, and walked over.

'Hello, Clara,' he said. He had known her, had stood in line to dance with her at Fort Halsey back in the days when there weren't five white women in all the miles between Sheep Hills and the Musselshell. 'Were you looking for somebody?'

She'd been tense and hard-jawed, but being called 'Clara' in a way that renewed a forgotten friendship made her soften a trifle. 'Yes. Yes, Tom. I was looking for Creighton North.'

He didn't ask why or show the slightest curiosity. 'He's not here but I think I can find him. Why don't you have a chair outside on the porch?'

She walked out with him. All the chairs on the porch were taken, and men were lounging against the wall and pillars. Nenus spoke to a man who got up quickly and carried his chair over.

'I don't want to deprive you,' Ma said.

'You aren't depriving me, Mrs. Wolverton. I been loafing all day.'

She tried to see his face, but when she did it wasn't familiar. The country, she noticed, was more and more filling up with strangers. Still, she felt more at home there, at the hotel, in the midst of the Association men than she would have among the sodbusters and haywire ranchers who had their rigs drawn up around the Apex. Live to be a hundred, she'd always have contempt for men who took up land under the Homestead Law.

She waited about ten minutes, listening to fragmentary conversation, suspecting the talk had been changed since her arrival. Then she saw North coming with Tom Nenus.

'Here's Cray, Mrs. Wolverton,' Nenus said, and without further comment went through the door.

North took off his hat, but there was no real courtesy in his hard jaw and narrowed eyes. He hated the Wolvertons, as Ma knew, but there were men watching from down the porch and he tried to hide it by smiling and saying, 'You're looking well, Ma.'

'I'm not feeling well,' she said, holding her voice down. 'I'm sick at heart to see the way things have stacked up.'

'*I* didn't make the choice.'

'It could be I blame you, and it could be I don't. That wasn't my purpose in sending for you. I sent to tell you I was ready to accept your offer for the ranch.'

'Oh.' He put his hat back on and scratched at the hard bristle of whiskers along his jaw. 'I'd have to get in contact with the head office before taking that up with you. I just work for the Great Western, you know; I don't own it.'

His answer seemed to stun her. She fought down a tremble in her voice. 'You're saying the offer is no longer open?'

'It's no longer open.'

'Then how much are you willing to pay?'

'We have no offer at this time.'

She said: 'I see. I hope you thought over just what you're doing.'

'I'd thank you to say just what you mean, Mrs. Wolverton.'

She gestured outward, at the street and at the knoll where half a dozen cookfires were blazing. 'That's what I mean. All those men out there. There'll be trouble tomorrow unless we settle on something. Maybe you think you'll take over the Flying W range anyway.

125

Maybe—'

'Let's not fight that over again.'

'All right. I'll not fight it over. I just want to say nobody'll win if it comes to range war.'

He said coldly: 'If there's range war, I'll not take the blame for it. I've stayed within the law. I've had cattle stolen and a man killed. I've just reached the end of the rope, that's all.'

With that he turned and strode inside. Ma was up, about ready to follow, but the screen door slapped shut in her face.

North crossed the lobby. He knew he was being watched, and he maintained a rigid control over his emotions. There was no apparent change in him, but anger had drawn his nerves taut and set up an inward trembling. During his earlier years, when he was a dirt contractor on the N.P., and later a freight boss with Musselshell, his temper had become notorious, and he had been known to relieve himself by striking the first man he met. He still carried a forty-four bullet behind his hipbone in memory of such an encounter. Of late years, however, he had learned the necessity of control, at least while his actions were under the scrutiny of men like Nenus and Major Eaton. So he satisfied himself by ramming space for himself at the bar and drinking a big slug of whisky.

While standing there he saw Nenus in the mirror, but he didn't turn until Nenus asked,

'Did she want to make some deal about Holly?'

'No.' Nenus was waiting for him to say what Ma wanted, but North didn't volunteer anything. 'Have a drink?'

'Not now, thanks. We'd better go up and see what the Major wants.'

They climbed two flights and rapped at one of the large corner rooms. Eaton himself opened the door. A three-burner oil lamp made it seem unusually bright. Inside with the Major were Barry Simmons of the Rocking R and a portly, theatrically handsome man with hair the silver of pussywillow.

Major Eaton, holding his panatela cigar delicately, said: 'Judge, you and Tom have met, I believe. This is Creighton North of the Great Western. Creighton—Judge Rakestraw.'

They shook hands, Rakestraw saying, 'Good evening, sir,' with practiced senatorial resonance.

Eaton offered a drink, and when it was refused, cigars. He called for extra chairs. There was some pointless small talk while the Negro boy went for them.

Seated, Major Eaton said, 'Barry and I have been explaining our position to Judge Rakestraw, but I'm afraid we haven't been very convincing.'

Pent-up violence broke through North's tone when he said, 'What d' you mean?'

Eaton showed a slight annoyance. 'I told

127

him our position in regard to Holly Wolverton.'

North, with the fresh-lit cigar damped between his teeth, called Holly a vile name.

Eaton said, 'This is a meeting among gentlemen, Cray!'

North laughed. 'I never had much practice being a gentleman. If you didn't want the judge shocked, you should have thought of that before you sent for me.' He addressed Rakestraw. 'You know, if I'd had my way, we'd never have arrested him. A stiff rope on a cottonwood limb, that's my idea of rustler medicine. The country's getting civilized, they tell me, and that sort of treatment's old-fashioned, but I'm not so sure. It's permanent, and it never cost the taxpayer much money.'

Rakestraw wanted to take North's words as a joke, so he laughed, without doing a very good job of it. It was hot in the room with the lamps burning. Sweat lay in droplets across his forehead. He shook out a handkerchief and mopped them away.

North said, 'Just what about our position hasn't been convincing, Judge?'

'Speaking, ah, entirely off the record, and among friends, I fail to see that you have a very good case. Against Wolverton.'

'You listen to *this* case! I represent Great Western. If you'll look over your books in Helena, you'll see we pay a hell of a lot in taxes. It's outfits like ours that make jobs like

128

yours possible. I think we're supporting the government better than the government supports us, and I'm getting fed up with it. I'm through sitting by, watching my profits melt away to outfits that register a brand, go into the mavericking business, and finally get so cock-full of fight they'll ride into town and shove you off the sidewalk like they did today. I'm sick of it and I'm through with it. Now, Wolverton's one of the worst. He's a horse thief and a brand runner. I want him sent up for twenty years.'

Rakestraw said, 'Are you trying, sir, to dictate to me my decisions in a court of law?'

'No, I'm not. You can do what you want. But if it doesn't measure up to my idea of justice—'

Eaton said, 'Cray, watch yourself.'

Rakestraw asked, 'If he's a rustler, as you say, why has the prosecution failed to mention it?'

'He's a clever one. He doesn't run brands into his own Flying W. He has a renegade deal with Drumheller across the river. He runs them into a D bar H, or one of the fifteen other brands Drumheller has registered, and splits with them. He had a hundred steers like that in the Drumheller tally last fall, and he rounded up another two hundred on our range not a month ago. That's why my cowboy was killed—because he wanted to bring a marked steer in for identification,'

Rakestraw said incredulously, 'You're telling me that *Drumheller* has been making deals with brand runners?'

'That's what I'm telling you.'

'Well, Mr. North, I must say! If you have proof of such a thing, *of course;* but such a charge against Drumheller . . . I'd be careful of many things before bringing such a charge—'

'I'm bringing no charge. I have enough fight here without dragging a big outfit like that into it, but I'm telling you, in private.'

Rakestraw thought about it. He shook his head positively, saying, 'Oh, this is a mistake!'

North had been tilted on the rear legs of his chair. He let himself forward with a bump and shouted, 'No, it's not a mistake!'

Rakestraw was obviously frightened. He mopped more sweat off his face. 'Your trouble with Drumheller is, of course, one which will have to be resolved through mutual agreement,' he said, groping for the correct words. 'I have no power, in the absence of criminal or civil action. Beyond mediation, that is. Mediation which I will freely offer, at some less pressing time, of course. My concern tonight must be strictly with the case at hand. On its merits. And this would appear, from my position, a neutral, an outsider if you will, to have greater ramifications than any of us have touched upon. Ramifications, ah, beyond my vested powers. Also, according to my observation,' he made a motion indicating the

130

crowd outside, 'the sentiment is by no means one-sided. You must consider that it is the duty of my office to protect not only property, a point which you brought out in mention of the tax burden, but also to protect the individual.'

North laughed with contempt and said, 'You mean you're being influenced by that gang of nesters?'

'I mean nothing of the kind. It is the duty of a court to explore both sides. That will be done. If Wolverton chooses to deny the charge, I will have little choice except to select a jury, however small the chance that twelve unprejudiced men can be found.'

'Maybe you'd even go so far as to turn him loose!'

'Perhaps, sir, that shall be done. If so, please do not hold me responsible for your own blunders. I understand he is to be charged with murder. Yet, according to my information, the very man he killed was wanted for the same charge in the Territory of Wyoming.'

'What the hell difference does it make what a man does in Wyoming? Half the men in this territory came here on the jump from a sheriff.'

'Alvis Brewer was a notorious gunman. That fact will have a bearing on the case whether you and I like it or not.'

North looked down in his perspiring face and said with sneering contempt, 'The truth is, you want to be elected governor and you've had time to count noses.'

Rakestraw, for a moment, lost the power of speech. When he regained it, he changed his mind about answering North and turned to Major Eaton. 'Sir, will you be so kind as to give me my hat?'

North shouted, 'No, you're not going until I tell you a few things.'

Eaton got hold of North's arm, saying, 'Watch your tongue!' but North shook him off and blocked the door.

'If you think I'm going to sit back and be hamstrung by a carpetbagger while a gang of rustlers—'

'North, be quiet!' Major Eaton's voice was like a saber through the room, and this time North, with an effort, checked himself. He walked to the window, stood with night breeze billowing the curtain against his legs, and filled his lungs deeply. He stood until Rakestraw was out, with the door closed.

Major Eaton then managed a thin smile and said, 'Anyhow, Cray, you let him know how things stand.'

Simmons asked, 'You think he'll have guts to turn Wolverton loose?'

'I'd interpret his remarks that way.'

North said: 'I hope he does. It'll be better that way. I'll kill that rustler when he walks out of the courthouse. I'll kill him, and I'll wager a thousand in gold that dirty-shirt nester army outside will sneak off without firing a shot.'

Simmons said, 'We'd better think this over.'

North laughed in a bitter manner. 'We've been thinking it over for eighteen months now,' and without waiting to hear anything else he strode from the door.

'Let him cool off,' Eaton said when Nenus rose to follow him. 'I'll talk to him in the morning.'

*   *   *

The courthouse of Grant County had never progressed beyond the stone foundation laid in the fall of 1886, and court was held in Tatum's Saddle Shop, two doors down from the jail. Every bench in the long front room was filled, and a mass of men blocked the entrance when Joe got there with Ma next morning. There was some jostling as a way was opened for them, and Wasey Stager, seeing them from the back room, came out carrying a chair for Ma. Joe stood with his back against the wall behind her.

It was still only nine o'clock, but the sun beat against the side and flat roof of the building. The interior seemed stifling. After getting his bearings, Joe looked over the crowd. Neither North nor any of his gunmen were there. Carslyle and old Billy Buzzard were the only members of the Association he saw, though riders from the big outfits were well represented. It did not make him feel easier that North and his gunmen were not around. If they started anything, it would not be in the courtroom. They'd be outside, waiting for Holly when he came to the door.

An hour dragged past. The crowd became denser, piling up along the walls, overflowing the platform walk outside. Finally, Judge Rakestraw arrived. He had a portmanteau which he unbuckled and searched for some legal papers. Finding them, he sat down and read for several minutes. At last, he nodded to the clerk, John Timmons. Timmons in turn said something to Wasey Slager, who went out the rear door and came back with Holly.

The manacles on Holly's wrists were removed, and he grinned at Ma, but some of the hell-and-be-damned air was gone from him. He had had his hat on, but now he held it tightly in both hands while hearing Timmons in his cultured brogue announce the case of *Montana Territory* v. *Hollis Wolverton* on the charge of murder.

The prosecutor, W. T. Hansard, an ungainly, tall man of fifty, thereupon arose and engaged Rakestraw in a long-winded, intricately technical discussion so couched in Latin that no one, with the possible exception of Timmons, knew what they were talking about. Finally, after leafing through a calf-bound copy of the *Revised Territorial Statutes,* Rakestraw cleared his throat for attention and said,

'After extended study of this case, the court fails to discover any reasonable foundation of the charge it has pleased the prosecution to submit . . .'

As he went on talking, and as it became apparent that he was throwing out the case for lack of evidence, a murmur arose. He struck the table with his gavel and raised his voice, concluding almost in a shout, warning Holly sternly against appearing again on a similar charge. That done, he sat down, wiped his forehead, and nodded to the clerk.

The crowd was milling, everyone trying to move in a different way, and getting nowhere. Ma shoved her way forward and reached Holly. She threw her arms around him, and Holly, laughing, lifted her off the floor. Chad Newhall, Horseshoe Conners, and Elton Stellingworth had been seated on the front bench, and now they were up, standing between Holly and the crowd, on the watch for trouble.

Chad said to Joe, 'You better get your Ma out the back door.'

Joe cried, 'I'm staying here! If there's any trouble, I'm—'

'Get her out!'

Joe took her by the arm and said: 'Come on. We're supposed to go out the back way.'

She said, 'Holly coming?'

He didn't know but he said, 'Yes.'

Dad Tripp came from the back room with a

sawed-off shot-gun over his arm and said something to Rakestraw, who was sorting papers from his portmanteau. Rakestraw shook his head and started beating the plank table with his gavel.

Dad said: 'You better quit chopping wood and let me get you out of here. We're likely to have trouble.'

'I have no fear of this mob.' He kept beating with the gavel. 'Sheriff, have your deputies clear the courtroom.'

While Joe was urging Ma to the rear door, he heard Holly say, 'I want that gun you took away from me, Dad.'

Ma also heard him and tried to stop, but the step was beneath her foot and with Joe urging she had to take it or fall. Then, when she was outside, there were men behind her and she could not go back again.

Joe kept pulling at her arm. 'Ma, let's get to going. We got to get the broncs hitched up. We got to get Holly out of town before things bust loose.'

She said, 'All right,' and started off almost at a run. 'You don't think Holly will do anything foolish, do you?'

'Dad Tripp'll take care of things.'

Going the back way, around sheds and rubbish heaps, they reached the Apex Stable. He shouted for the hostler but no one answered. He cursed through his teeth. The team was in one of the square plank corrals out back. Working with nervous speed, he got halters on the horses, led them out, and backed them against the wagon trees.

Ma said: 'I'll finish with the team. Get Holly's horse out of the barn.'

Holly's sorrel was tied in a stall. Joe tossed the saddle on him and crowded in to pull the latigo tight, then mounted, got the tie rope loose, and rode at a gallop down the runway through the big front door.

From there, at a slight elevation, he could look down the street. Everyone seemed to be gathered around the courtroom door. Holly hadn't made his appearance and no trouble had developed.

He eased back on the reins and rode at a swift trot, eyes hunting for Creighton North. Neither North nor his men were in sight. He would have felt better if they had been.

Dad Tripp came through the door, the sawed-off gun in his hands. He swung it in front of him in horizontal arcs and advanced, making room for himself and the men who followed him. Slager and the eight deputies, regulars and specials, started clearing the platform walk. While they were about this, Holly sauntered through the door.

It was the moment Joe had thought about and dreaded. He expected a volley from some unexpected quarter. Seconds strung out one after another and nothing happened. His horse came to a halt, frightened by the crowd, and reared a couple of times against a tight bridle. Joe noticed that Tripp had not given Holly the gun.

Ma had hitched and was just now driving around from the rear of the barn.

The crowd kept falling back as Tripp shouted at them. Holly was in the middle of the walk, with Newhall on one side and Stellingworth on the other. Down in the street, leading two horses, working against the crowd, was Jake Stroop, once a bartender but now a homesteader on Goosebill.

'Holly!' Joe could hear Stroop shouting. When that failed to attract Holly's attention, Stroop called: 'Chad, send him down here. I can't get any farther.'

Chad apparently relayed the message, but Holly didn't move. He wasn't running. He was giving the Association its chance.

Joe noticed that the up-street members of the crowd had turned their eyes in a new direction. He looked and saw Creighton North, flanked by Tripplett and Garfield, walking rapidly down the platform walks. North was tall, and he kept making himself taller by craning his neck and occasionally boosting himself high on the crest of a step to glimpse Holly.

Joe wanted to shout, but excitement tied a knot in his vocal chords.

A rifle shot shattered the hot morning air.

It had long been expected, too long, and

now it had the unexpected impact of a bolt of lightning. Its first effect was to stun the crowd. For a second there was only a surprised milling while echoes rushed back from the false fronts. Then men stampeded in every direction.

The sorrel started to buck. Fighting him too hard, Joe turned his neck and almost made him fall. His back was toward the two-story St. Louis Café, but from the corners of his eyes he caught a glimpse of a man reeling high along the edge of its boxlike top. He turned as the man took his third stumbling step and dived with limp arms toward the street. The man turned over as he fell, disappearing among men and horses. The crash indicated that he had struck a hitch rack. A blue-roan bronc broke away and galloped through the crowd, wall-eyed with fright.

Someone else on the roof of the St. Louis was firing, and he was answered from half a dozen quarters. The crowd melted away and Joe found himself alone in mid-street. His horse, after bucking and making a full pivot, was now on a gallop while bullets stung the dirt behind and in front of them. Joe finally got him behind Sullivan's blacksmith shop.

He dismounted, drew his forty-four, and ran back to the street corner of the building. He checked himself and peeped through the notched log projections. No one was left in the open. He could see men lying in the protection of sidewalks or in the narrow passageways

139

between buildings. A deadly sing of bullets tore up and down the street.

After a time the shooting died, and he saw Dad Tripp and his deputies near the jail. Dad, with his shotgun hung in his arm, strode gangling and long-legged to mid-street, where he turned in a slow pivot to look at both factions. He stopped with his back toward Joe and shouted: 'Eaton! Major Eaton, do you hear me?' Joe couldn't hear the answer, but Tripp's voice had a high, carrying note as he went on. 'Eaton, you keep your men down there!'

This time he heard Eaton answer, 'Sir, we did not start this!'

'You keep 'em down there!'

Half a minute passed with no shooting. The deputies were now all in mid-street, forming a loose group, facing different directions. Dad said something to Wasey Slager, evidently leaving him in command, and walked as fast as he could, without running, toward the Apex Stable, where about twenty men of the homesteader faction had formed a nest among cast-off wheels and wagon boxes.

Others commenced showing themselves here and there, but the mid-section of town was deserted. Beyond Hong Gim's hand laundry Joe saw Elton Stellingworth. He ran back to his horse, mounted, and risked crossing the street to catch up with him.

'Elton!' Joe called. 'What happened?

140

Where's Holly?'

Stellingworth tilted his head in the general direction of the north road, saying, 'Yonder.'

'Who got killed?'

'Mean that one on the roof? He was some ace-in-the-hole of North's. Heard somebody say Hoffman. I don't know. That was nice shooting, wasn't it?'

'Did you—'

'No. Not me. Don't tell anybody, but one of the Dumas boys got him. He had one of those old Sharps singles and he shot him off at 250 yards. Holy hell, that's shooting!'

He saw Ma and rode to her. 'Holly's yonder someplace—'

She said: 'I know where he is. We better leave town.'

Joe tied the sorrel to the end boards and got to the seat beside her. When they were jouncing across the bridge, Ma said: 'Who started that shooting? Who was it shot that man off the roof?'

He couldn't resist a little swagger in saying: 'I don't know. What difference who knocks down a bushwhacker?'

'It wasn't you, Joe?'

'No, it wasn't me. It was one of the Dumases. But don't say anything.'

She muttered, and kept muttering: 'I do wish it had been them that started it. I do wish it had been them!'

CHAPTER TEN

As they drove northward, the rigs from homesteader outfits along the Goosebill fell in with them, but the trouble everyone expected did not materialize. At nightfall, when they reached the home corral, Holly was there, roosting on the top rail, waiting for them. He had a horse roped and ready for his saddle.

'You leaving already?' Ma asked. 'Why can't you stay with me just a little while?'

'Now, Ma, don't get that tone again.'

Ma walked to the house. She was sitting in her favorite chair, her high-button shoes off, letting her feet breathe, when Joe came. 'Saved from the gallows, and he won't even stay with his own mother for supper.'

'You know they'll be out gunning for him now. He has to leave.'

'He wasn't too scared to show himself in town.'

Two days later eleven-year-old Billy Newhall rode over bareback with news that Art Gamey's gang had utilized the excitement in town to stage a horse raid. They had got away with an estimated two hundred head of remuda stock from Great Western, Rocking S, and Goosebill.

Billy wound up his account by saying, 'My mother sent me over so Holly would know.'

Ma barked, 'Why'd she think Holly should know?'

He looked scared. 'I don't know. She just said that. She said maybe you and Joe ought to stay at our place for a while. She says there's bound to be trouble.'

'I lived here since before you were born and I never asked for protection yet.'

When Billy rode off, Joe said: 'You shouldn't have talked to him that way. The Newhalls were just trying to be decent.'

'Blind-bridle outfit!' she muttered. 'I don't like teaming up with their kind.'

'You don't like teaming up with anybody.'

He started for the corral and she called, 'Where you think you're going?'

'Out to find Holly.'

'Why?'

'If there was a horse raid, Holly'll get blamed for it whether he was in jail or not,'

'Holly can take care of himself. I got too much work to do around here for you to be chasing off all the time.'

He mended corral all afternoon. That night, when the house was quiet, he slipped out through the window, saddled, and rode northwestward as far as Wing Coulee. There he changed his mind about going to the Coalbank line shack and angled back to Newhall's. At the edge of Thirty-Mile Coulee, still a mile from the ranch, a woman shouted, 'Stop where y'are!' and he came to a stop with his hands high and wide from his body.

The woman's voice had sounded familiar, and now he remembered whose it was. It belonged to Bill Johns's wife. 'Who are you?' she asked.

'Joe Wolverton.'

She climbed into sight over the edge of a little dirt cut, shoving a rifle ahead of her. She was dressed in levis, a faded shirt, and boots with the sides ruptured. A better outfit could have been picked up on a Box Elder rubbish heap.

She said: 'Seems like you're always sneaking around by the dark of the moon. You'll get shot that way.'

He grinned and pushed his hat back so that he would look like Holly. 'And *you're* always on hand to do the shooting. What are you doing *here?*'

'We came over to stay with the Newhalls.' She laughed in her high, unsteady voice, adding, 'We figured the Newhalls didn't have enough kids already.'

'How many are shacked up down there?'

'Don't ask me to count 'em. I never got through my fifth frame. I better go down to the house with you. Jake Stroop's on the lookout someplace. He's itchier on the trigger than I am. Laws, after getting you and your brother out of town alive, I don't want you should get shot now.'

'You must be expecting trouble.'

144

'After that fight in Box Elder? Of course there'll be trouble. They got the names of every man that was in town, and they won't rest easy until they run out every one of 'em, or try to. But I don't care. I told my man to go, and I'm glad I did.'

Jennie Newhall, a plump, cheerful woman who still looked pretty after ten children, heard them at the corral and was up and dressed when they reached the house. There was no floor, only swept dirt, and children slept on straw ticks everywhere, two and three to a tick. Jennie lit the bacon-grease lamp, built a fire, and made coffee, talking all the while, but none of the children awakened.

She said, 'We were hoping maybe Ma would come.'

'Burn that old house over her head and she'd be back camping in the ashes. Anyhow, nothing'll happen to her.' He looked in the other room, expecting to see Chad asleep in the bed, but it was empty and tumbled, showing that Jennie had been there alone.

She saw him and said: 'You looking for Chad? He ain't been here in two days. I heard your voice and thought it was Holly. I figured maybe they'd come in together.'

'Where'd they go?'

'That's something I figured to ask you.'

He ate, slept, and waited until afternoon, hoping they'd come. Then he rode to the line shack.

145

No one was around. There was day-old manure in the corral. All the wood had been used up; the stove, completely cold, was filled with ashes; and rancid sardine cans had been left on the table and floor.

He stayed at the cabin, not leaving for more than two or three hours at a time for fear Holly would come. On the third afternoon, hunkered in the shade of rocks on one of the hill flanks, he saw a lone rider picking his way along a trail from the direction of Gros Ventre Springs, and even through the shimmer of heat wave at two miles he knew it was Holly.

He called to him and rode down. He noticed that Holly had another new hat and that the gun at his hip was a new one with mother-of-pearl stocks.

Holly saw him eyeing the gun. 'How you like it?' He drew it and tossed it to him. 'Here, take a shot with it.'

It was a forty-five caliber Colt, nickel-plated and covered with floral engravings. The pearl stocks were cross-etched so that they clung to a man's hand. Joe thought it was the most beautiful gun he'd ever seen.

'Go ahead and shoot it,' Holly said.

Joe spotted a soda-white heap of dirt at the mouth of a prairie dog's burrow. The gun had a balance and feel that seemed to make it aim itself. He fired and saw the responding geyser of dust dead-center on the heap.

'You aim at that?' Holly said, looking at him

narrowly.

'Sure.'

'Well, I'm damned! Hit it again.'

There was nothing to it. The gun seemed to aim itself. Holly said, 'Well, throw away that old forty-four you've been carrying and stick it in your holster.'

'I won't take your new gun.'

'Take it and be damned. It's no good to me. I couldn't hit a bull in the rump with it across Ma's kitchen.'

Holly stayed at the shanty only long enough for supper, then he roped himself a horse from the bobtailed remuda Joe had gathered at the corral, and jerking his head at the badlands, said: 'I got to drift over yonder. Don't know as you ought to stay here by yourself, Joe. Why don't you get Ma and take her over to Chad's?'

'You don't think they'd get rough with Ma!'

'Most of the Association wouldn't, but North would try anything.'

'When you coming back?'

'I'll be here tomorrow, late. Think I will. If I'm not here by night, don't stick around any longer. I'll see you at Chad's.' He called over his shoulder: 'And keep clear of the cabin. North finds out you're sleeping here, he'll ride up and riddle it.'

Joe slept in the brush up-creek, waking every hour or so to listen. In the morning he took up his old place on the ridge. It was another blistering day. Summer had long ago dried the prairie until its grass crunched under a man's boots. Heat rose in waves as though from the top of a stove, and mirage like fire kept rolling in from the east, disappearing, changing to lake, and to lake with mountains rising from it. The light so abused his eyes that half the time he kept them closed.

Toward the end of long afternoon, he saw a rider coming along the prairie rim from the general direction of Newhall's. Heat wave distorted both horse and rider out of proportion. The horse had a giraffe look; the rider could have been twenty feet high. The horse was a bay or a black. The rider seemed to be wearing a pair of wide-winged chaps. The horse was being pushed at an alternate trot and gallop, a killing pace through such an afternoon. He kept watch for many minutes as they neared and shrank to proportion. What he'd taken to be chaps was a reddish-brown riding skirt. The rider was a girl—Ellen Eaton.

She rode around to the cabin door and leaned over to look inside. Seeing no one there she turned and scanned the corrals. He shouted, and when she failed to turn, started to shout again—it took that long for his voice to reach her.

He sensed that she was a trifle scared, and knew why. So he called, 'Its me, Joe!'

When he got there, she was holding her sweat-streaked bay in the partial shade of the corral.

She said, 'Joe, are you alone?'

'Yeah.'

'Where's Holly?'

'I don't know.'

'Isn't he staying here with you?'

'No.'

He swung down beside her. She looked tired out. Dust had formed gray circles under her eyes and around her lips. He guessed why she was there even before asking and hearing her answer.

'The Association is on the howl. Dad's men, North's, the rest of them.'

'You mean they're headed *here*?'

'I don't know. I don't know where they'll go. They're looking for Holly, and that bunch from the badlands too, but for Holly most of all. They'll kill him if they find him, Joe.'

'Where are they now?'

She shook her head. 'Dad and six of his men pulled out this morning. I heard him talking to Alf. They planned to meet North and his riders at Eagle Point. Probably they'll come straight here. I was lucky to beat them at all.'

As she talked, her eyes kept roving the ridges; Joe began to watch them, too.

She said, 'Joe, you got to find him.' She got hold of his shirt. With her so close, he forgot all about Holly. She was looking up into his eyes. She seemed on the point of crying.

She said: 'He can't stay any longer in this country. They won't give up till they kill him.

It'll only be a question of time. My dad's always wanted him dead. Now he has the excuse, and all the others will be backing him.'

He said: 'Don't talk to *me* about it. You're the real reason Holly won't leave the country.'

'Oh, Joe, that's not true! If he cared anything about me, he *would* go. I've told him that. Honest I have. I told him if he really cared anything about me he'd go someplace and make a start for himself. I won't even be here in another month. Dad's making me go back to Helena.'

'You like him a lot?'

'I hate him!' The words surprised Joe until he realized she meant her father. 'Yes, I do! I hate him, and I think he hates me. I might as well be a prisoner, here and in Helena both. He won't even let me go to dances. If he ever found out I rode to Box Elder that night, he wouldn't let me leave the house for weeks. And if he ever found out that I came here—' She didn't finish. 'Anyhow, I don't care what he'd do. Someday I'll leave and never come back. I'll leave him just like my mother did.'

She was crying, her lips pressed, her small chin set; crying without a sound, tears streaking through dust on her cheeks.

He felt sorry for her. He wanted to say something. He felt helpless and awkward.

She moved away suddenly, saying: 'I'll have to go. I can't let him catch me here. Joe, please find Holly. Make him get out of the country.'

Her horse was completely beat out. He roped a fresh bronc for her, swapped saddles. It took ten minutes.

'Where you going?' he asked.

'I don't know. I guess back to the ranch.'

She'd just taken the reins when her eyes were attracted to the ridge. He looked and saw movement where the trail climbed up from one draw and dropped into another.

She swung to the saddle, but the bronc, frightened by the quickness of her movement, almost bucked her off. Joe got hold of the bridle and fought the animal down.

'Ride straight down the creek,' he said. 'Keep in the water. Then take the trail up that draw to the east. Just a second. I'll ride with you.'

He mounted and led the way. In a hundred yards the brush closed in. For a long time they had to ride doubled over, with twigs ripping at them. He found the trail, watched her out of sight, and then climbed in the opposite direction, along a steep side, through dirt creviced by erosion. He left his horse in the concealment of a bullberry thicket and went on afoot with his rifle across his arm.

Lying on his stomach, he looked down on the camp. Men were there now, poking through the sheds and pounding the creek brush. Many men. He tried to count them, but more kept coming. He guessed at forty. Someone stepped outside the cabin, and even at that distance some characteristic in his movement told Joe it was Creighton North.

North waited as mounted men gathered around him. He talked and gestured repeatedly in a northerly direction, toward the badlands.

Someone rode up from the creek driving a horse ahead of him. It was the bay Ellen had been riding. Joe felt sick, for he knew that Eaton would see his own brand and guess how the horse had got there.

He lay with his forehead pressed on the hot ground, cursing himself because he hadn't driven the horse down-creek. It was late now. It was too late even to warn Ellen. When he looked again, they were riding northeastward. Now he counted them. There were forty-three. They were headed toward Art Gamey's, he had no doubt of that. It was a better than even bet that Holly wouldn't be there, but he couldn't take the chance. He'd have to get there first and warn him.

When they were out of sight, he went back to his horse and rode down the creek into the badlands. The creek became a trickle and sank away in the earth. He kept down the rough coulee bottom until twilight came. When it was dark, and there was little chance of being sighted, he climbed to the ridgetop, remembering that Holly had said that it would lead him straight to Gamey's.

The country had a massive unfamiliarity

after dark, but when the moon rose he recognized landmarks. A cool damp wind came from the river. The thirsty horse was willing to run, so Joe gave him his head. At an alternate gallop and trot he struck the eastward-trending valley. The bottleneck cliffs were there, with Gamey's place just beyond. He watered his horse in the tiny creek and rode on warily. He wondered if he should fire his gun as Holly had, then he decided against it. He stopped, cupped his hands and shouted. The echo of his voice came back. He shouted again and again without receiving an answer. He was still about four hundred yards away. He edged closer, watching for movement. Then he was startled by a man's voice that seemed to be right at his elbow.

'Who are you?' the voice had asked.

Joe jerked around. He couldn't see him. He had been deceived about its nearness. The voice had come from the black shadows of cottonwoods forty or fifty yards away.

Joe said, 'I'm Joe Wolverton.'

'Holly's brother?'

The man sounded relieved. Joe had the feeling that one of them had been as scared as the other.

'Yes. Is Holly in there?'

'I don't know. He is unless he lit out along one of the back trails. I left before dark to stand watch. Who's with you?'

'Nobody.'

Suspicion reappeared in the other's voice. 'The hell there ain't!'

Joe had been riding toward him at an easy jog. Finally he saw him—a tall, blond kid, probably no more than seventeen. He had a rifle over his arm, ready to shoot, and there were two pistols tied down to his skinny thighs. He was walking to meet Joe, and the weight of the guns interfered with his movements. He had a horse somewhere, blowing and shaking his bridle, but Joe could not see him.

Joe said: 'I tell you I came here alone. I got no time to fool around.' He thought of something that made his stomach bottomless. 'Who'd you think came with me?'

'I seen something.'

'Where?'

'Yonder.' He motioned toward the summit of the narrows and toward the ridge that backed Gamey's house. 'I was just goin' to start over and warn the boys.'

He was lying. He suspected an attack and had been afraid to go back inside the valley.

Joe cried, 'The Association was headed this way with forty-three men; that's who you saw!'

The blond kid, watching the high rocks, saw something. Without warning, he tossed the rifle to his shoulder and fired.

The bullet struck and pinged away. Seconds later a volley came in answer. Joe could see the spaced-off flashes of three guns. A bullet left the scorch of its nearness against his cheek. His horse, frightened, was already running.

The drop-off to the creek was suddenly in front of them. The horse stumbled head first and rolled completely over.

Joe was down among rosebushes with stems half as thick as his wrist. He was groggy for a few seconds, trying to get movement back in his muscles. Thorns had ripped his clothes and gashed him. Their pain was like fire. He was suspended a foot or so from the earth. He fought back, leaving ribbons of his shirt behind. There was much shooting now, farther away, inside the narrows. It came in waves, volley on volley, with little one- and two-second gulfs of silence between. He had arrived too late. The attack had been set and sprung.

He still could not quite get his wits about him. He took a step, knew he was exposing himself, got down again. He had lost his rifle. He waded thorns, stumbled against the gun, and picked it up. He wondered about his bronc. He did not want to be afoot in the badlands. The blond kid was nowhere around. He decided to cross the creek.

Rose thorns formed an almost impenetrable wall. On hands and knees he managed to claw his way through; then he dropped down the perpendicular bank and was halfway to his boot tops in water. He could walk there, bent over, with bushes bowered above. After blind

155

travel he came to a crossing and stopped to see what his chances were.

He no longer had hope of catching his horse. Ahead, through a rift in the brush, he could see some of the shacks and corrals. Attackers had taken positions along the ridge. Others had circled to a grove of cottonwoods across the coulee from the corrals. He kept moving up the creek. When brush played out, he crawled on hands and knees. Water stung when it touched the thorn wounds on his hands and arms. He passed through the narrows without drawing a shot.

He stopped when it became apparent that following the creek would take him within short range of the cottonwoods. He couldn't reach the cabins; he couldn't help in any way. Now that he had taken the chance, he could see no purpose in it. He should go back, try to find his horse, and get word of the attack to Newhall's, to home; but he could not move as long as he had an idea that Holly was one of the men trapped in the cabins.

He hunkered on his muddy bootheels, watching the fight shape up. Some of Gamey's men had crept out and were shooting from the corrals. The sulphuric odor of powder smoke came drifting on the night breeze. After fifteen or twenty minutes the gunfire slackened. Whole minutes went by with only a shot or two.

A ball of fire that he at first took to be a

shooting star arched from the ridge and struck earth between two of the shacks. There it lay and burned with a smoky flame. A kerosene-soaked rag had been wrapped around a rock, lighted, and flung by means of a sling.

A second one came. It arched but fell short. A third struck the slope, bounded, and rolled, leaving a trail of flame in the grass, then thudded as it struck the logs of a cabin. More and more of them appeared. One commenced to burn in the roof of a hay-covered shed. The flame barely maintained itself for ten seconds, then suddenly it took hold and raced with almost explosive rapidity. It lighted the valley. In another minute or so one of the cabins was burning too.

Shooting burst with concerted fury as men made a run for the corrals. He could see them briefly. They found cover and opened fire on the Association men in the cottonwoods. They had a momentary advantage, then attackers closed in from the ridge. It had given them time to saddle their horses. They made a break for it. He heard the fall of the corral gate, the thunder of hoofs, the whooping and shooting as they raced up-coulee through cross fire. Most of them got through, but an unexpected volley met them a quarter-mile farther along, at some narrows. He could no longer tell one side from the other. The fight seemed muddled, a scattered, furious mix-up.

He heard the high, carrying voice of

Creighton North: 'Alf! Get your men along the cutbanks before they crawl through the draws. Let's kill every damn' one of 'em!'

It made him sick. He stayed down, and could not help being thankful that the fight was drifting away from him. Fire kept spreading from one shed and shanty to another. Despite the brightness he risked climbing up from the creek. No one seemed to be closer than half a mile. He started back down the trail, running until the weight of his waterlogged boots stopped him.

He sat down, emptied his boots, and put them on again. He kept going, on the lookout for his horse. He made a turn in the coulee, then another. The fire was a distant glow over flanks of the ridge, gunfire was a far-away popping. After getting his breath he became aware of the night stillness. Even the gunshots did not disturb it. The loudest sound was the crunch of grass under his boots. It was like that for a mile or more, when suddenly the movement of a horse startled him.

It was his bronc with the bridle tangled in rose thorns.

Joe stopped and sat on his heels for a while, not wanting to frighten the animal. Then, talking in a quiet voice, making no sharp movement, he reached in his hip pocket for one of the bits of hard sugar he always carried there and advanced with his hand outstretched while the bronc, with flanks aquiver, waited for him.

He felt better with the bridle in his hands. It occurred to him that a man was only half a man without a horse under his pants and the weight of a gun at his hip. He still did not know quite what to do. He rode back slowly. He waited while the horse picked grass, rode on little by little. The night passed, and the stars were commencing to fade. For a long time now there had been no shooting; or if there was shooting, it was so far away it left him uncertain. Some riders appeared up-coulee and came at a gallop, passing on the other side of the brush without seeing him.

Sighting the narrows, he started up a switchback game trail that had been dug from the northern cutbanks. It was so steep he had to dismount and go ahead, pulling the bridle. The crest of the ridge was narrow and steep. He dropped over it. There, getting his breath, he peered down on the burned-out shanties. The long sweep of coulee seemed to be deserted.

He kept riding, stopping to watch, riding again. He dropped down the steep path to a feeder gully, and there, two miles above Gamey's, glimpsed three men hanged to the outstretched limb of a cottonwood. The sight turned him sick and sweaty. He wanted to turn his back, but an awful fear that one of them was Holly kept him from doing so. The hanged men were an eighth of a mile away, shadowy against the deeper shadows of a cottonwood grove. There was no way in which he could identify any of them. Trying not to think, he rode straight across the bottoms. His horse became frightened and tried to turn away, but Joe controlled him on a tight rein. At thirty steps he drew up. The faces of two dead men were visible but neither was Holly's, neither was familiar to him. A hat had been pulled down over the face of the third. It wasn't Holly's hat and the boots were different. He got his breath, then. Sweat was running down the sides of his face. He mopped it off with his shirtsleeve.

Given his head, the bronc moved swiftly up the coulee. A man had been shot and was face down with his boots sticking from a clump of sagebrush. He rode over and saw that it was Jack Noe, the short, blond fellow who had been seated with Garfield on the day that North had tried to buy the ranch. He kept going. At a brushy turn in the coulee a man called to him. He drew up and swung around. His hand lay on the checkered stocks of his new gun without drawing it. He thought the voice was Holly's, but now he wasn't sure.

'Yeah?' he called.

'Here, Joe. And get out of sight.'

It *was* Holly. He had no feeling for danger; he was too relieved to hear the voice and know he was alive.

Box elders with a dense undergrowth of

rose and buck-brush lay in front of him. 'Where are you?'

'Down here in the brush. By the big box elder.'

He dismounted and led his horse. Finally he saw Holly, propped on one hand, his Colt on the ground beside him. He was naked to the waist. He had torn up his shirt and wrapped it around his middle.

Joe said, 'You hurt?'

'Little scratch. I'd have made it all right, but my horse threw me.'

It was an effort for Holly to speak. Joe got a better look at him. He was hurt worse than he pretended to be. The wound was evidently in the right side, near the base of his ribs. Joe swung down and walked to him. Holly tried to get up, but his braced foot slipped in the dirt and Joe thought he was going to collapse. He ran and got his arm beneath his shoulders.

'I'm all right, Joe, I'll make it all right on my own. All I need is to sit down for a second.'

'You're hit bad, Holly—'

'Oh, the hell I am. I've taken slugs like this before. It cracked a couple of ribs and went on through. I'd have made it out of here on my own, only when I try to walk it bleeds. That's the chief thing I'm scared of, losing blood.' He hunted his pockets. 'Got the makings?'

Joe fashioned a cigarette and lighted it for him. Holly smoked rapidly, without taking it from his lips, which trembled so much that the

161

ashes dropped off.

Sounds became audible—the slight brush crackle of movement. It made Joe go tight inside. He imagined it was men on horseback. He glanced at his bronc, which was nibbling brown pennants of buffalo grass unalarmed. He breathed again, and in a while his pulse slowed down. It was only the scurry of cottontails or prairie chickens.

'Think we're all right here?' he asked.

Holly moved suddenly and opened his eyes. 'Damn, I been asleep? Why'nt you wake me?'

'You only been sleeping a minute.' He asked again, 'You think we're all right here?'

'I don't know. They took out after Chad and that bunch down toward the river.'

'Were you in the house?'

'Yes. Say, were you watching that? What in hell are you doing here, anyhow?'

Joe told him about Ellen's visit to the shack. Holly made no comment.

'How we going to get out with one horse?'

'I'll walk,' Joe said.

'We can give it a try, but you'll have those boots broke in when you're through.'

Joe tried to rebandage the wound, but the fabric had stuck tightly and he couldn't get it off without hot water. He took off his own shirt.

'Here, put this on.'

'What'll you do? The sun'll come up and fry you like a pancake.'

162

'I'll make out.'

He intended to go back to take a shirt off one of the dead men, but once by himself he couldn't do it. Instead, with breeze feeling cool and good around his naked skin, he climbed several cutbank pitches and crouched in a clump of sage to watch and make sure no one was coming. Then he went back and helped Holly into the saddle.

Holly uttered no sound, but Joe could see by the pale set of his mouth how much it hurt him. Using Holly's cartridge belt, he cinched him tight to the pommel.

'All right?'

'Sure.' Holly managed a grin. '*Now* look who's going back to Ma roped over the back of his horse!'

They started up the coulee, Joe leading the bronc along a trail that skirted the brush. He was tense for a few hundred yards, then the rhythm of steady movement had a lulling effect and danger became like a dream, far away, something left behind with the night.

Dawn was ahead of them, hunting out some clouds that were invisible before, coloring their undersides yellow and red. The brush played out and the coulee narrowed. Sage grew to a man's waist. It was dusty dry at that season, and as they walked through it the smell rose in suffocating waves.

After long nodding with movements of the horse, Holly jerked and said, 'They're coming,

163

Joe.'

Joe stopped and reached for his rifle while his eyes traveled along the ridges.

Holly managed a laugh. 'It's a mite long range for that old forty-four. They're yonder, beyond the cottonwoods.'

Men, trotting their horses, filed into sight. They dropped through a little dip and came to view again, about three-fourths of a mile away.

'They see us,' Holly said.

Joe felt trapped. His eyes, looking for escape, rested on the toadstool rock that marked the coulee turnoff.

'Ride straight past it,' Holly said. 'They'll lose sight of us in the cottonwoods. Then we'll double back.'

Joe set off at a run, still leading the horse. He kept watch over his shoulder. The Association men had spurred to a gallop. He kept going until they dropped from sight in the cottonwoods. 'Now!' Holly said, and Joe turned sharply back to the coulee.

His boots gave him trouble. Their heels, never made for walking, kept toppling under him as he crossed rock and tufted grass. His heels became raw. He wanted to stop and straighten his socks, but time was too important. He kept looking back over his shoulder. They must have traveled for half an hour. The sun rose and became hot, with still no sign of them. He noticed that Holly had rocked far forward, both eyes closed. A stain of fresh blood had worked through the bandage.

He stopped and said, 'Holly!'

'Yes?' His voice had a vacant sound, as though he didn't know where he was.

'You all right?'

'Sure. How far are we along?'

'We must be almost there.'

'Almost to Chad's?'

'No. Almost to the cave. Thought maybe you could tell me.'

Holly still didn't seem to be in his right mind. His eyes moved around without coming to focus. 'I don't know. This country looks all alike when you wake up in the middle of it. Just keep following these bottoms. You'll come to the cave all right.'

Joe stopped again at the next turning. He listened. In the distance he heard the clack and echo of a hoof on rock. He had put his rifle back in the scabbard, but now he drew it out. He speeded to a swift trot, keeping it up until the steepening grade of the bottom winded him. Back of him, for three hundred yards, the coulee lay in a straight line. He got Holly out of sight, and waited, leaning against a shoulder of dirt.

The sounds were much closer now. He could hear the hoof thud and clatter of other horses. The sounds faded, grew louder again. He worked the lever of the Winchester, saw the glint of the cartridge in the barrel, closed it. He'd have to shoot from close to the bronc's head or trust Holly with the reins, so he knotted them and got them through his arm. He guessed at the distance and elevated the sights. All the while he watched, listening to the sounds as they bore down on him.

Three horsemen burst into view, almost side by side. Others were coming. He tossed the gun up and, taking a general aim at the group, pulled the trigger. The bronc, frightened, pawed back and almost flung Holly from the saddle. Joe was dragged three or four steps, but he saw the bullet kick dirt low and to their right.

The lead riders came to a sliding halt. One of the men had pulled up and was sidewise toward him. He thought he recognized Red Tripplett, but it was too far to be sure. He fired again, aiming higher by the height of a man. This time the dust puffed beyond them, from a bank of yellowish clay. It was close enough to start them milling for cover.

He let the horse drag him out of sight. Holly was shouting: 'Give me the reins. You can't shoot that way.' He got them off his arm and put them in Holly's hands. The bronc was nervous, but he'd got over the desire to buck. Holly asked, 'Where are they?'

'Down past the turn.'

He climbed up the shoulder of dirt, stopped at a little crest about thirty feet above the floor of the coulee, and propped on his elbows beyond a shale outcropping, fired the magazine dry.

Bullets flew back, but none came closer than a dozen feet. They stopped shooting. He had no further sight of them. He reloaded and counted the cartridges in his belt. He had about thirty forty-fours left and ten forty-fives for his new pistol.

The riders were again in view, about two hundred paces farther back, getting their horses up the steep eastern side.

Holly was calling to him.

'I'm all right. Just seeing what they were about.' He slid down, heels first, jumping the last ten feet while dirt showered over him. 'They're headed up the side, east.'

'Let 'em. They'll run into trouble following that ridge. They'll never head us off now.'

The stop had let him recover his wind. He kept up a steady running pace for the next half-mile, then it was another half-mile of switchback to the cavern passage. Holly had to dismount there. He seemed to be steady enough until his feet touched the ground, then his legs collapsed and he fell forward on hands and knees. He rolled over and sat up with enough strength to push Joe away. 'Go ahead and get the bronc through. Blindfold him. I'll get some life worked up in my legs by that time.'

Holly was on his feet when Joe returned. He was able to walk through with one arm around

Joe's shoulders.

It was late morning then, perhaps ten or ten-thirty. The sun on the barren eastern slope was hot and brilliant. Joe could feel it burning his body. He stopped, got the saddle blanket, and cut a hole through which he slipped his head, making a rude poncho. Holly was asleep, sagged forward with his hatbrim touching the mane of the horse. When they started forward, he rocked and almost pitched to the ground. Joe had to snub the stirrups and then tie his boots down. They went on and on, down the vast slope, across bottoms as dry and hot as smelter slag.

In the baked bed of a creek he stopped and took off his boots. His heels were blistered, and the blisters had broken. His socks had worked down in the boot toes. He got them out. Big, ragged holes were worn in the heels. He put them on, the heel side over his instep, and bound his feet with strips torn from the bottom of the shirt Holly was wearing. The boots went on hard, but they felt better.

He went on, trying to remember landmarks in a country of monotonous sameness.

His lips were bitter from sweat salt and alkali. Thirst tortured him. He no longer watched for pursuit. From a slowly climbing trail he looked for one of the bright splashes of green that would indicate an ooze of spring water, but there was none. In all the vast, heat-shimmering country there was only grey earth

168

and rock blending with a blue-white sky.

At times the country would seem familiar. He couldn't be sure. He crossed one ridge and then another. The sun lay as much south as west, so he kept it at his back, maintaining a course that would take him out somewhere near Chad Newhall's. Finally, beat out from heat and thirst, he stopped beneath the lean shadow of a cliff and started to untie Holly's feet.

'Give me a drink,' Holly said, husky and thick-tongued.

'Here, let me get you untied.'

Joe tried to help him down, but Holly fought him off and fell as he had at the cavern. 'Where's the water?' he kept saying.

'You'll have to wait.'

'Why?'

'We'll have to get to Thirty Mile.'

Holly raved and cursed. He called Joe names. He was feverish and irrational, obsessed with the idea that his canteen was on the saddle and that Joe was hiding it from him. Finally he played himself out and, lying on his side, seemed to sleep.

Joe sat with his back propped against a boulder, hatbrim resting on his eyebrows, and watched the back trail. His eyes kept blurring from lack of sleep. He slept in spite of himself, and awoke with shadows lengthened and the brutal heat of afternoon gone.

Holly was awake, watching him. He seemed

169

rational now. Joe spoke with an effort, making words come from his thirst-sticky mouth. 'How you feel?'

'Pretty good. I sure could use a drink,'

'I ain't got any. We got no canteen, Holly.'

'I know it.' He evidently remembered nothing about the struggle Joe had had with him. 'I been thinking I'd like to drown in that big spring pool up at Gros Ventre. How'd you like to stick your head in that, Joe? Just stick your head in and never come up.'

'You feel like traveling now?'

'I feel pretty good. You know where we are?'

'Thought maybe you did.'

'We'll ride and have a look around. How far we travel from the cavern?'

Joe had no idea. He got Holly on the horse and tied his boots down again. They traveled through late afternoon. There were no landmarks, just barren hills and steep gullies. Darkness settled and the country changed, looking cavernous and mountainous, as it always did when shadows filled it. The moon rose, and they went on and on, up coulees without end, until at some lost hour of the night they climbed a final steep pitch and were on the rim of the prairie.

Joe tried to get his bearings. The Coalbank Hills were farther away than he expected. He'd come out to the east of Chad Newhall's instead of to the west.

170

Holly roused himself and said: 'How'd you get way over here? This your private trail? We better head for Stellingworth's. That's his coulee over yonder.'

Stellingworth had settled on land midway between Thirty Mile and the Goosebill. It was not more than three miles to his place, while it was five to Newhall's and almost ten to the home ranch.

Now that the end of the trip was near, Joe got on behind his brother and rode double. Approaching the coulee, he smelled wood smoke. Drawing up along the rimrocks, he saw that a fire had swept the place earlier that night. All that was left of the house and sheds were glowing rectangles where the thick base logs of the walls were still unconsumed. He wasn't surprised, alarmed, or angry. He'd taken too much abuse. He was just thirsty. He wondered briefly if Stellingworth, a bachelor, had been killed. There was a spring back of the house. He hoped no Association men were around to keep him from it.

Holly was asleep, and Joe didn't awaken him. He dismounted and led the horse down successive pitches of the side. There was a wagon road below, but a layer of brush barred him from it. He was too fagged to hunt for a trail. He tried to force his way through. Briers cut his skin, ill protected by his saddle-blanket poncho. The bronc, tangled, refused to go on. Joe turned back to hunt a new course. He saw

171

movement down the road and heard the drawl of Ned Garfield's voice. He forgot his thirst and stopped, holding the bronc just below the bit. Other voices came to him. Men were on their way up the wagon road. The brush was above his head, but through openings in it he was able to guess their number as twelve or fourteen.

A voice he didn't recognize was saying: '. . . down in Maverly, but that was before he met up with Liz. She ruined him. He never touched a drop in those days.'

'Liz was all right,' Garfield said.

He had a brief, clear view of the lead rider's silhouette against some alkali patches in the coulee bottom. It jolted him to realize that it was North. He had imagined that North and his men were behind them, following their trail through the badlands.

The others kept discussing somebody he'd never heard of, when North's voice cut across the talk, saying: 'All right, look sharp! Somebody might have heard the shots and come from Newhall's. If they did, the chances are they'd lie low along here. We don't want any eye-witnesses turning up. We're likely to have trouble with Nenus as it is. Red, maybe you and Dean better cut the road and swing up around that way. Wait in one of the dry washes and see if we jump somebody. We'll fan out and work these little draws.'

Garfield said, 'Just like chasing cattle.'

A voice he didn't recognize said: 'What'll we do when we jump 'em? Rope 'em and brand 'em?'

'We branded *one* tonight!'

Several men laughed, but North didn't laugh; he had an ill tempered answer. Hearing him, Joe could picture the underslung jut of his chin.

Garfield said: 'Those kids over at Newhalls would be the likely ones to come snooping around. I'm having no part in killing kids, Cray.'

There was a raw edge to North's voice when he answered, 'I'm not out on pleasure!'

Once before Joe had sensed the clash of personalities between North and Garfield. He held his breath, waiting for Garfield's answer that didn't come. They were so close now he could hear the squeak of saddle leather, the quiet jingle of bridle links.

His bronc jerked and blew. Joe got a head hold and muffled him. He listened, tense, his teeth set, using all his strength on the horse. The wagon road was a scant hundred feet below. They passed and kept passing, riding singly and by twos. It seemed to take a long time. Finally, with the last sound of them gone, he let up on the bronc and remembered to breathe.

Holly's eyes were open and he spoke in a dead-tired voice: 'Who was it? North?'

'Yes.'

'Looking for us?'

'They been burning Stellingworth out. I think they killed him.'

He didn't know why he was sure of that. Someone had said something, and it led him to assume that Stellingworth's body was inside one of the burned-out buildings.

He waited for fear one of them would double back along the rims and see them. At last he got the bronc around to a game trail and down to the road. A cribwork of half-burned logs fell as he approached the remains of the cabin. It sent up a new burst of flame. He made a wide circle of the light, skirted the corrals, and reached the spreading apron of mud and water that came down from the spring.

Holly smelled water and with a crazy laugh tried to get off the horse. He found his feet lashed and fought to free himself. He kept cursing and struggling while Joe tried to reason with him. The horse was drinking avidly from one track after another, leading Joe ankle-deep through mud. Finally he cut Holly loose with his clasp knife and tried to help him dismount. Holly twisted away from him and fell full length. He found a water-filled depression and drank.

'Not there, Holly! Come in to the barrel.'

Holly kept gulping water. Failing to make him listen, Joe climbed through the pole fence Stellingworth had built around the spring, lay on his stomach, and drank from the old vinegar barrel that had been sunk there. At last he forced himself to stop. He'd heard of men killing themselves on cold water after a long thirst. He thought of Holly and got back through the fence. Holly who had rolled over to his side, was resting, with muck and green scum dripping from his face.

Joe said, 'You better not drink any more cow tracks.'

'It's wet.' Two words at a time were about all he could string together. 'This is—good stuff. Same color as—Kentucky whisky. Better'n 'at damned—whisky.'

After a rest Joe caught one of Stellingworth's workhorses, mounted bareback, and rode with Holly to the ranch. They got there just as the sun sent its first yellow blaze over the horizon. It had taken them exactly twenty-four hours to get home.

CHAPTER ELEVEN

All seemed to be quiet. Ma was up, he knew, because a breakfast spiral of wood smoke rose from the chimney. He had intended leaving Holly somewhere and riding down alone to see if everything was safe, but now he changed his mind and went straight down across the shallow creek and barebeaten ranch yard, drawing up just outside the pole awning.

From inside he heard Ellen Eaton cry, 'Oh, Ma, it's Joe, and he's got Holly with him.'

He was too tired to be surprised at Ellen being there. It made him stiff to ride the broad-backed workhorse Injun-style. He got off and turned his attention to Holly. Ellen and Ma were both asking questions at the same time.

He said, 'He took one through the ribs. He'll be all right with a little rest. Let's get him to bed first. I'll tell you all about it.'

They helped him to get Holly inside. He hit the bed, exhaled, and lay like a dead man. Ma took his clothes off, cut as much of the bandage away as she could, and commenced soaking off the rest with hot water. Ellen helped, and when her help was no longer needed she stood with a hard clench on her emotions, looking down in Holly's face.

'Who was it?' she whispered to Joe. 'Who did it to him? Was it my dad?'

'I don't know. It was all of 'em. They burned out Gamey, hung some men. I found him wounded in the brush. Got out to Stellingworth's. They burned him out, too. Killed him, I guess.'

'My dad did that?'

'No, he wasn't with them. It was North and his gunmen that burned out Stellingworth.'

Ma said: 'Quit telling something you don't know. How you know who killed

Stellingworth?'

'I was there and saw 'em ride away!' He'd held in too long. Fear and fatigue had burned him out, and now, at home, he was ready to give way to his emotions. He wanted to lie on the floor and cry. To keep from it he raised his voice in anger at Ma: 'Why you still want to pussyfoot around North? I ain't scared of him.'

'You say you saw 'em?' She gave Joe a hard look, wondering if he'd spoken the truth. 'If you did, all the more reason you shouldn't say so. They won't want any witnesses. Once they've started on the kill, it'll be easy to keep going; you'll only put yourself on their list.'

Holly opened his eyes and said: 'Sure, Joe. We know who burned him out, but we aren't talking about it.' He smiled up at Ellen and closed his eyes again.

She said, 'Hadn't we better get a doctor?'

Holly's lips moved: 'No, a doctor would just lead 'em here. They'd hang me if they caught me. I'll have to get patched up and leave the country.' He hunted Ma with his tired eyes and smiled, whispering: 'Ma, where was all this Injun land you said they threw open? I sure would like a look at it.'

Joe had a drink from the bucket. He was weak from hunger. He ate a huge breakfast and lay down on the bench to rest for a minute.

When he woke up, the midday sun was blazing outside. He sat up with sudden alarm

177

and peered from windows at both sides of the house, but everything was quiet. He looked around for the new gun Holly had given him. Someone had put it on the table. He strapped it around his waist and glanced inside Holly's room. Holly was asleep, his mouth open, snoring a little. His skin looked dry and leathery, like an old man's, but his breathing was good. No one else seemed to be in the house. No sound. Only the snoring, and the heavy fly drone of early afternoon.

He tiptoed outside and met Ellen Eaton. He said, 'Ain't you been home at all?'

'No.'

'Your dad knew you came out to the line shack.'

She looked scared. 'Are you sure?'

'He saw your horse. We forgot and left him by the corral.'

'He didn't know I was riding that horse. I got him at our Circle Springs camp.'

'He wore the Goosebill brand and there was sweat on him. Your dad's no fool.'

She said: 'I don't care! I'm never going home!'

He wondered if she intended to leave the country with Holly. He wanted to ask her but couldn't. Instead he asked, 'Where's my rifle?'

'I don't know. What are you going to do?'

'Keep watch. Somebody has to.'

'You don't think they'll come *here*!'

'Sure they will. They're out to get him.

They're out to get all the small ranchers.'

'Joe, you can't stop them alone!'

'I'll stop some of 'em alone.' He started away and turned. 'Where's Ma?'

'Out gathering wormwood for a poultice.'

His gun was in the scabbard, hanging with his saddle down in the shed. He got it, found two boxes of forty-fours, filled all the loops of his belt, and distributed the rest through his pockets. While he was about it, Hap Williams cut off the light in the door.

Hap said, 'They burned out all the little outfits along Goosebill, too. They burned out Bill Johns with the kids right in the house.'

He looked in Hap's eyes. 'Who told you *that*?'

Hap blustered, 'Don't you believe it?'

'I just asked who told you.'

'Halfbreed I run onto over by the stage road.'

Joe pretended to believe him, but he didn't. Not even North would burn kids in their house. Hap was always thinking up lies like that and getting angry when they weren't believed. Anyhow, the Johns were camping at Newhall's.

Hap said, looking at the cartridges, 'Where you going now?'

'Up on the hill to keep watch.'

'What'll you do if they come? You ain't going to fight 'em off all alone.'

'All right, then—get your gun and come

along. I'm not letting them take Holly.'

Hap whined, 'I got some things to do for Ma, or else she'll—'

'Get your gun and come along!' Joe shouted.

Suddenly Hap was scared of him. He could see it in his eyes. 'All right, Joe. If you say so, Joe.'

They spent all afternoon on a low bluff overlooking the ranch and Gros Ventre Creek. At sundown Joe saw men approaching. By their number he knew it was not North's group but those led by Major Eaton.

They came at a good clip, but when they were still beyond rifle range the two lead riders pulled in and the rest gathered around for a conference. After three or four minutes they spread out and formed two main groups. The two who had been in the lead were still closer than the others by forty or fifty yards and came riding straight down the wagon trail that would lead to the house.

Joe slid the rear sight to its top elevation, aimed a few feet ahead of them, and fired.

The bullet evidently came closer than he intended. One horse reared in a half-pivot and almost threw its rider.

Instantly, by apparent prearrangement, all the riders came to a stop. Falling back, one of the lead riders, whom he could now recognize as Major Eaton, got his arm high for another conference.

They sat around talking for many minutes. They were at it so long that Joe slid back along the little V-cut gully, where he found Hap crouched and scared, with his rifle across his knees.

He said: 'You keep watch along the creek. They might try to send some of 'em up through the brush. Keep firing and moving. It'll be twilight in a little while, and maybe they'll think we got a lot of men and will leave us alone.'

'All right,' Hap whispered.

Joe wondered if he really had any fight in him. Ma had heard the shot and was outside with a shotgun in one arm, her other arm lifted to shade her eyes. Ellen stood in the doorway behind her.

Ma spoke over shoulder, evidently telling Ellen to get back. Then she crossed the yard, her eyes still hunting the brush-filled gullies that cut up from the creek.

'Joe,' she called. 'Where are you, Joe?'

For a while he pretended not to hear. She wouldn't want to fight. She'd try to make another deal with the Association. Finally he said, 'Here I am.'

'Who you shooting at?'

'Eaton and his Association killers.'

'How many are there?'

'About twenty.'

'Hap up there with you?'

'Yes.'

'All right. You keep 'em off as long as you can. Keep 'em off till dark. I'll see if Holly can travel.' She started back to the house, stopped, and called: 'Don't let 'em surround you there. If they start pressing you, get to the barn and I'll back you up.'

He was wrong about Ma. She had plenty of fight. It sent a warm feeling through him to have her talk that way. He said, 'We'll take care of 'em all right!'

He moved back between the steep sides of the gully. They were still out of range and seemed to be watching the north-east.

A bulge in the prairie prevented his seeing what it was, but a dust haze had risen and hung yellow as corn meal in the sunset. More riders were coming: North and his men. They'd been down in the Goosebill, burning the small outfits as Hap had said.

He lay low, waited. Little by little the Association men kept falling back. He lost sight of them. At last, through late twilight, a lone rider came over the prairie bulge, his horse at a wary amble, a white handkerchief tied to the barrel of his rifle.

He stopped about two hundred yards away and shouted, 'Wolverton!'

He knew the voice. It belonged to old Billy Buzzard.

'Don't try any tricks, Billy!'

'This is for your good more'n mine.'

'All right, come along.'

Billy put the rifle away and rode the remaining distance at a lope. Joe, with his gun ready, climbed out to meet him.

'Hello, Joe,' Billy said. He cantered to a stop and sat leaning over his horse, a gray, pale-eyed little man, looking at Joe and down at the ranch buildings. 'Joe, boy, I know how you feel, but this time you're cutting yourself more trouble than *you* can chew.'

'That's my business, ain't it?'

'Why, yes. I guess it is. Only we ain't meaning *you* any harm, Joe. You nor Ma, neither one. You're an old-time outfit. You should be on our side instead of against us. Those nesters will whack this country up with barbed wire and plant turnips, and it won't be good for anybody.'

'Why you here if you don't mean us any harm?'

'We're looking for Holly.'

'What do you want of him?'

'You know well enough, Joe. We saw you riding away from Art Gamey's with him. He's been rustling cows and horses both for better'n two years, throwing in with Gamey, and you know it. Maybe you been too, Joe, but we talked it over and are willing to overlook—'

'He's not a rustler. He never—'

'You put a halter on that temper of yours, Joe, because it's not going to do any good. He was shacked up with Gamey. You know it, and I know it, and the Association knows it'

183

'You're asking me to hand him over?'

'We'll give him a trial, Joe. That's a promise.'

'The same trial you gave those three you had hanging to the cottonwood down in the badlands.'

Billy considered this while rolling a cigarette. He was a quiet-tempered little man whom everybody liked, and it was hard not to like him now. That's why they sent him. Joe knew that, and he steeled himself against being swung over by any promise Billy would make.

Billy said, 'What if I guaranteed, personally, that he'd be taken in to the jail and kept in sheriff's custody?'

'How *you* going to make a promise for Cray North?'

It was true and Billy knew it. 'All right, Joe. If you want it the hard way, we'll come down there after him.'

'How you know he's here?'

'We know he is, that's all.'

'He's across the river, fifty miles away, headed for Canada?

'No, Joe. He's there.'

Joe heard something and suspected that they'd sent Billy to occupy his attention so that others could come along the creek. He spun with his rifle ready.

'It's me!' Ma shouted from below. 'Who's with you? Billy Buzzard?'

'Yes.'

Billy would have ridden down to talk to her but she said: 'Stay put. I know what you got on your mind. You think to look around and see where we got our men placed. Well, you'll find out soon enough when you try and smoke us out. You go back to those timber-wolf pals of yours and tell 'em that. You may have us outnumbered two to one, but by clang that's just how a Wolverton likes it!'

Billy took the cigarette out of his mouth and let his eyes search the creek. 'Outnumbered two to one' would mean the Wolvertons had fifteen or eighteen men cached in the bottoms, and it was evident that he more than half believed her.

'I wasn't trying to spy. I offered to come when nobody much wanted me to. I was just trying to save some lives.'

'Us Wolvertons never asked for favors. Now get out o' here or I'll buckshot you and your white flag both to ribbons.'

Ma watched him ride away. When he was out of earshot, she said to Joe: 'You better come down. He was giving you a good look-around and he'll have the lay of the land. If I was you, I'd first hole up in the root cellar and then pull back to the sheds when need be. Where's Hap? Did he take it on the high lope?'

'No, I never took it on no high lope!' Hap said in an aggrieved tone from the edge of the creek. 'I never shirked a fight in my life.'

'You're pretty deep in the brush to do much battling right now.'

'I'll fight as much as the next man. It's only that I ain't as young as I used to be.'

'Then you haven't got as much to lose. You talked gun-fight for the last twelve year, and if—'

Joe said, 'Leave him alone, Ma.'

Joe stayed there until late twilight. Ma came back to the house after leading a saddled horse down past the old garden patch. It would be ready there in case Holly needed to make a run for it.

Joe said, 'Time to move, Hap,' and led him to the root cellar. The root cellar was a roofed-over cave sunk in a little rise of the bottoms where it would be away from seepage water. Deep enough for a man to stand upright in, it was filled with the moldy smell of fermented turnips and potatoes.

Joe poked some chinking from between the logs, and leaving Hap there, walked on to the shed.

Darkness settled with heavy bullet-colored storm clouds that rolled in from the southwest. Lightning played along the horizon. It seemed humid, with the dead, breathless feeling of still air before a storm. He looked at his gun. The barrel and action were badly fouled after the shooting he'd done the day before. He drew oiled rags through the barrel. Then there was nothing for him to do except wait.

It was quiet. Occasionally, from the darkened house, he could hear Ma's voice as she said something. He kept thinking that they didn't have a chance, five against thirty, or more than thirty. And the five included old Hap, and Holly, who was wounded, and Ellen, who had hardly fired a gun in her life.

The moon, rising, made a silvery line at the prairie horizon, but storm clouds soon moved around to cover it. A wind sprang up, rustled the wilted leaves of box elders, loosened some of the dried hay that covered the roof. Memory of the kerosene fireballs made him nervous, but if they set fire to the shed he could always reach the blacksmith shop with its roof of poles and dirt. At first the wind had an odor of heat-scorched prairie, then suddenly it was cool, filled with the smell of freshly dampened dust. Hunkered in the rotted hay and manure that softly padded the dirt floor, he rolled a cigarette and dry-smoked it until it was a sodden lump between his lips.

A flash of lightning, closer than the others, sharply revealed a man who had just slid down the face of a cutbank less than eighty yards up and across the creek. The glimpse was momentary, and the darkness after the lightning seemed more intense than ever. Joe let the cigarette fall and rocked forward on one knee with the rifle up. Then he saw the man again, a shadow against the white gumbo face of the bank. It was too dark for the sights, but instinct brought them level with his eye and he fired.

The man was hit. He knew that instinctively, even before he heard the startled grunt and exhalation of his breath. After a few seconds of shock, while the gunshot echoes bounded away, the man commenced crashing through brush, cursing, and grunting with effort after every word.

A man shouted: 'Larry! Larry, you damned fool!'

Another said, 'Grab him!'

There was a struggle. They were trying to drag him back to cover. Bullets smashed the shed from two directions, none of them close. He shot twice more at the concentration of men that seemed to have developed near the cutbank. Hap was firing too, and guns were speaking from the house.

He kept moving, shooting at gun flashes. Bullets hummed up and down the length of the horse shed. He bellied through the side door, outside, past the wreckage of an old wagon, and inside the blacksmith shop. He continued to shoot and reload. The old rifle, spitting powder again now that the oil had been burned out of it, blinded him. He shot awkwardly, left-handed. Lightning flashed every eight or ten seconds, giving him repeated glimpses of creek bottoms, of bent-over trees with the gray undersides of their leaves toward him, and he saw the occasional shadow movements of men. They had moved as far as they could in the cover of brush, but none of them took the chance of crossing the final seventy to a hundred yards of coverless bottom.

Finally it was apparent that the first attack had petered out. He stopped firing. Everyone had stopped firing. Rain blown at a long angle by wind looked like millions of silvery wires each time the lightning flashed. Through the glassless window at his back, a cold spray entered and covered him. The wind became cold, as though from snowfields. Hail had fallen somewhere. At last the rain stopped, the wind eased off, and thunder, after coming close, drifted away and became a heavy rumble in the north. It was very dark. They'd be coming again, now, and he didn't know any way of stopping them.

'Joe!' He could hear old Hap, quavering and scared. 'Joe, can I come over there?'

'Stay where you are.'

'Damn it, I'm the first one they'll get at.'

'Oh, all right, but keep down.'

After a long wait he heard Hap's voice in the shed: 'Joe, where you at? I can't see a thing in here. It's blacker'n a gambler's heart.'

'Stay there. I'll be over.'

The ground was slick from rain, but it had sunk down less than half an inch. A slight breeze was blowing but it was no longer cold, merely damp and fresh. Despite danger, it was good, after long drought, to smell the rain on grass. He stood in the partial cover of the side door, filled his lungs, and with Hap calling again, crossed at a doubled-over run without drawing a shot.

Cloud breaks in the east were silvered by the moon. The storm had blown itself out. They'd have to attack inside of ten minutes or lose the advantage of heavy darkness.

'I'm clean out o' ca'tridges,' Hap's voice said from the blackness.

Joe gave him a handful. He groped through the storeroom and found another box.

He said: 'Go easy on 'em. We only got another fifty.'

Hap felt better, now that the immediate danger had passed and Joe was beside him. He giggled and said: 'They sure scared up a hornet hole when they came in after us! By the sweet-scented hell we *did* blast the middle out of 'em. See that lobo that tried to slip past me on the up-crick side? I waited for him, holdin' right down for him to come into my sights, and when he did, *bam!* My old rifle turned him inside out like an empty Durham sack.'

'You killed one of them?'

'You damn' betcha I did! Only I think his pals drug him away. Reminds me of the time over on Jeff Davis Crick, other side of Bannack, I and some fellows from over Lemhi was sluicing bench gravel and some claim jumpers tried to tear down one of our flumes and—'

He was cut off by a blast of gunfire. It was on the other side of the shed, toward the house, yet not so close as Joe at first thought. He saw flashes of powder across a disused garden plot, from some downstream cutbanks, from the old caved-in shanty that his father had built when he first took the ground back in the seventies.

'Ma!' he called. 'Ma, where are you?'

There was no answer. The house seemed to be empty. Then, after what seemed to be a long wait, a single gunshot pounded from that direction. The moon slid into view. After long blackness the valley seemed very bright. He saw men on horseback along the crests, took a shot at them, and drove them out of sight. The fighting again slackened off. He called Hap's name but no one answered. Suddenly, fearing a stray bullet had killed him, he started along the runway. Hap then crawled from beneath a manger and started digging hay out of his shirt.

He said: 'This place is no protection at all. Lead goes through here like water through a funnel.'

'Well, get back to the root cellar.'

'I'm going to.'

He kept watch on the house. It seemed to be abandoned. The entire creek valley seemed to be abandoned. After a long wait he heard Ellen's voice just outside.

'Joe?'

He took a deep breath and stood in the door. 'Here I am.'

In some manner she had left the house and come up from the creek side without his seeing her. She was carrying a Colt revolver in her hand. It looked pendulous and out of place.

'You'll get shot,' he whispered. 'Come inside.'

She moved obediently. He had a glimpse of her face before the heavy darkness hid it. Her eyes seemed to be shocked and half-comprehending.

He said, 'What happened?' When she didn't answer, he had a sick, sinking sensation. 'Are they all right?'

'Ma's—up there.'

'How about Holly?'

'Didn't you know? Ma had a horse waiting for him down in the bushes. He got away.'

He leaned on the door. For a second relief from fear left him dizzy. 'You sure he was strong enough to ride?'

'Yes!'

She said it with unexpected force, almost defensively. She seemed to be crying. Her shoulder was against him, and he could feel the restrained, convulsive jerkings of her slight body.

'How about Ma?' he asked.

'She's all right. She told me to come here. She says I'm to stay here with you.'

192

'Why? What's she going to do?'

'I don't know. She thought my dad would find out about me being here. She wanted me to stay with you.'

Joe couldn't understand it. The fight had become muddled, without reason. The Association could wipe them out. He didn't know why they weren't doing it, unless they knew Holly had escaped and were following him.

He said, 'I'm going up there and find her.'

'No, Joe, no!' The thought of his leaving her seemed to fill her with terror. She clung to him even more desperately than she had that night at the hotel in Box Elder. 'No, Joe. Don't leave me. Please don't leave me. Ma's all right. You have to stay here with me, Joe.'

He felt sorry for her. With Holly gone, he had the feeling that he was the only friend she had left on earth. He wanted to take care of her, to keep her from her father, from everybody.

She still had hold of his arm. Under her urging he walked with her down the black inside of the shed. She groped and found the entrance to a box stall. Sacks of oats from last winter were laid in a slanting heap against the wall. She half tripped, sat down, and pulled him beside her.

She was still crying, fighting it back with clenched teeth, making no sound.

'Don't cry, Ellen,' he pleaded. 'He'll be all

right.'

'I know. Don't talk about it. Just stay with me, Joe. Don't talk about anything.'

'He'll get through, Ellen. Holly's got out of tight places before. He always lands on his feet.'

'Don't talk about it.'

'Ellen—'

'Just don't talk about it!'

She got her arms around his head and with a fierce strength pulled him against her bosom. He was aware of the frail structure of her body. He could hear the rapid impulse of her heart. Her cheek, damp from tears, was pressed to the side of his head.

He slid little by little down the sacked oats, and with her, moved to a new place. Then, in each other's arms, they were a long time without speaking. He was scarcely aware of time. All the fear and danger, and hatred of the last days were locked out. It seemed that in all the world there were only the two of them.

An hour might have passed—or two hours. A man's voice registered on his hearing. He disengaged from her arms and stood up.

'Joe, stay here—'

'I'll be back.'

He found his rifle in the dark and carried it to the door. The voice, coming across the night, was far away. He heard it again, and the clatter of hoofs over creek pebbles. The man was riding the other way, leaving. Ellen had

194

followed as far as the runway. Dimly a moon silhouette at the far door, he could see her brushing hay from her riding skirt.

He said, 'I guess they pulled out.'

'Stay here anyway!'

He couldn't say No to her. He didn't want to say No. He walked back with her, and they were together through the long hours until daylight.

CHAPTER TWELVE

Ma was up as usual to prepare breakfast. Her face was stony, and she kept her back turned when Joe tried to find out about Holly.

Finally he cried, 'Whyn't you tell me anything?'

'Because I don't want you tagging along after him. He got away; that's enough, ain't it?'

Hap came in time to eat. He wanted to talk about the fight, but Ma quieted him and they sat down to breakfast in silence. Neither Ma nor Ellen ate much. When the meal was finished, Joe took a long walk. Here and there he glimpsed the brassy shine of a cartridge, but there was little else to tell of the night's fighting. The valley, the prairie around, all was deserted, serene under the hot morning sun. When he got back to the corral, Hap was harnessing a team to the buckboard.

195

'Ma's taking her back to the Goosebill,' Hap said.

'Like hell she is!'

He walked to the house. Both of them were in the kitchen. He cried to Ma, 'She ain't going back there!'

Ma said gently, 'Joe, you ought to be able to see that she can't stay here any longer.'

'Why can't she?' He addressed Ellen. 'You ain't going back to your dad. You said yourself that you hated him.'

Ma said: 'He'll find out she's here and come after her. Then it'll be worse for her than ever. She should never have come here in the first place.'

Ellen said, 'Oh, Ma!'

'Not that I don't love you, child. I do. But you'd be better off if there'd never been any Wolvertons. You'll be best off now if you go away and forget about all of us.'

'I won't ever forget!' She was about to start crying again.

Ma said, 'Joe, go out and help Hap with the buckboard.'

Hap had just driven up. Ma took the reins from him, and Ellen got in the seat beside her.

Joe said to Ma, '*You* driving her clear to the Goosebill?'

'Of course. You don't expect me to send her back there alone, do you?'

Ellen said: 'I'll be all right, Ma. Dad probably won't even be home.'

'That may be and it may not. Anyhow, he'll know where you were. I let you stay, and now it's up to me to face him alongside of you. I never hunted an easy way of doing things.'

*   *   *

It was long after dark when Joe heard the buckboard rattle up the creek road. He stood in the window and watched Ma turn out the team and walk to the house. She was alone. In the morning he asked what had happened, but all she'd say was, 'It'll lead to no good when there's a feeling like that between a daughter and her father.'

He decided Ma and Ellen had had a rough time with Major Eaton. Later in the day he saddled and rode to Newhall's. He found Jennie sick from worry and with no word yet from Chad.

'He got away,' Joe said. 'I'm sure he did. Holly said that night he was headed for the river. Chad'll be back when things quiet down—just like Holly. The Association will find out we don't chase so easy.'

She didn't believe him. Some of her plump prettiness was gone. Her eyes looked large and dark-circled. 'No, they killed him. People keep telling me he'll be back, but I might as well face it. They killed him.'

He noticed that Mrs. Johns and her kids were there, so there'd been no truth in Hap's

197

story about North burning them to death in their shack.

He asked, 'How about Stellingworth?'

'You didn't hear? They killed him. Some of our men rode to his place yesterday and found him, what was left of him. He'd been shot and the place burned down atop of him.'

At a meeting that night Joe wanted to send someone through the Coalbanks and across the TN range to see Saxon and the Dumas boys. 'We'll never get anywhere with the Association as long as they got us split in half,' he said.

They agreed with him, but no one was willing to leave. He knew there was no real sentiment to do more than hole up and wait. With Stellingworth and Chad gone, they were licked. He rode away with some of Ma's feeling toward homesteaders rankling inside him. He headed for the home ranch, but only for a fresh horse, and he slept the late hours of night at a shanty on Dogtown Flats. Still with no real plan, he rode on, toward Box Elder, finally coming to a decision when he sighted the town that afternoon.

It was a quiet day. A supply wagon from the Rocking S was at the Barker platform being loaded with supplies, and a few saddle horses switched flies in the shade of cottonwoods by the Stockman's House.

He tied up in front of the sheriff's office, stepped inside, and paused to get sun blindness from his eyes. 'Dad?' he said, and getting no answer, walked on to look down the jail corridor. There were four cells on one side and a log wall on the other. It was rather cool but ill ventilated, filled with the smell of hay ticks and unlaundered blankets. Only one prisoner was there—a cowboy with a purple-bruised face snoring out the last end of a spree.

He heard the boot thud of someone entering behind him, turned quickly and saw Wasey Slager.

'Hello, Wolverton,' Slager said, making it sound friendly. 'What can I do for you?'

'Where's Dad?'

'He's not around.'

'That's not what I asked you.'

Slager chose to ignore the sharpness of Joe's answer. He seated himself in Dad's chair and took time to roll a cigarette. 'Sit down,' he said, lighting and blowing a cloud of smoke. 'I want to have a little talk with you.'

Joe sat down and waited.

'Why you always got a chip on your shoulder, Joe? Toward me, that is. I always liked you. You and your whole family.'

Everyone knew that Dad Tripp had named Slager his undersheriff as a concession to the Association. Joe wanted to say so. He wasn't afraid to say so; it was just that he didn't trust himself not to go on and say too much. While he fidgeted, Slager said:

'I often thought about you and Ma out there and what you must be up against. I know you won't believe this, Joe, but I wished to hell I could help you.' Slager offered to toss the makings. 'Cigarette?' he asked.

'Sure.'

Joe caught the tobacco and papers. He felt trembly. Slager, casual as he seemed to be, was closely watching him. It was as though Slager knew how nervous he was. He wondered if he'd be able to roll a cigarette at all. He waited a few seconds for his pulse to slow down. It seemed to him that Slager was smiling a little. It was a challenge now, and he couldn't back down. He remembered how Holly had rolled one that night of the Association meeting with perfect, frozen steadiness while his pulse beat in his throat. With what seemed to be a casual slowness, Joe opened the Durham sack. His fingers didn't tremble. Seeing that, he became confident and finished building the smoke. It made him feel good. It made him feel like a better man than Slager.

Slager went on: 'Of course, as undersheriff I couldn't do a thing, no matter how I wanted to. Dad nor me, neither one. There's only the two of us and two deputies. Hersey doesn't count; he's hired by the stage company. We couldn't get in the middle of the ruckus. I tried to make Holly understand that, and now I'm trying to make you. With luck, we got Holly out alive that day of the trial; but when the homesteaders and the Association get to warring along the breaks, there's nothing much we can do. Nothing anybody can do short of calling out the Army. I'm telling you this because you came riding in today, and maybe you want to drop a lot of trouble in Dad's lap.'

'Like what?'

'Like bringing charges on account of a killing.'

'What if I did want to bring charges?' He said it softly, and blew at the ash of his cigarette the way he'd seen Holly do in the past.

'It's your privilege, but look at it this way: you'll be putting Dad up against it and not helping yourself. And he's done his best for you. He saved Holly from getting lynched.'

Joe tilted back on the hind legs of his chair, the cigarette in one corner of his mouth, one eye closed against the smoke. 'Hangin' be damned! They didn't have guts to come for Holly in the open. They had a couple of bushwhacks planted on top the St. Louis. Only, *somebody else* got a whack at them first.'

Slager came to life, saying, 'Who was it fired that first shot?'

The cigarette froze in Joe's lips. 'I don't know.'

'You know all right, and—'

'Thought you were the one that couldn't be caught in the middle of this ruckus! So what difference who did it? Notice you're not interested in the ones killed on our side. Like Stellingworth. Why don't you ask me who killed him?'

Slager checked himself and sat back. 'Stellingworth? 'What about Stellingworth?'

'Dead. Burned inside his own house.'

'I didn't know anything about it. You better tell me everything you know.' He got pen and ink to make it look like business.

'Why don't you see North? He can give you the whole works. He can even give you Stellingworth's last words.'

'Joe, if you really know anything—'

'Oh, the hell with it.' He got up, yawned, laughed, and stretched himself. He was sweating so he had to pull his pants away from his legs. 'We're not getting anywhere. You better tell me where I can find Dad.'

Slager was standing, too. All pretense at friendliness was gone and he cried: 'No, you're not going to see Dad! I'm giving you just five minutes to get out of town.'

His sudden violence brought Joe around. He could feel the weight of the forty-five at his right hip and knew just where the butt lay—the mother-of-pearl butt of the gun Holly had given him. He could almost feel it in his palm, the way it fit, like no other gun he'd ever handled, and at that instant he knew as certainly as life and death that Slager was no match for him. He met Slager's eyes. He heard himself talking. He was surprised at his easy tone, at the things he was saying.

'Don't talk to me like that again, Slag. You look around, you'll notice that there's only the two of us here.'

He saw a quick shiftiness come to Slager's eyes. He realized that the man was bluffing and that now he was afraid. It lifted him, and for a second he felt lightheaded and giddy. He wanted to drive his contempt home with a laugh and a word or two, but one of Holly's remarks came back, that the man who did the most talking did the least shooting.

All that he said was, 'Now tell me where Dad is.'

Slager seemed to be holding his breath. He exhaled, and spoke from just behind his teeth. 'He's in his room. Upstairs in the hotel.'

'Thanks.'

He went outside. Turning his back gave him a creepy itch between the shoulders. He wanted to hurry. He had the almost uncontrollable impulse to look back through the screen door. He conquered it and walked with deliberate slowness down the platforms and gravel paths to the cottonwood-shaded hotel.

Soldier Jim and several other elderly men were seated on the porch. Jim saw him and cackled his ancient joke, 'Well, there's Wolverton and it's his night to howl.'

Joe laughed and went inside. 'Lost some

toes in the trap,' Holly had said. Joe felt as if he'd lost some toes in the trap. He didn't feel like the same fellow who'd gone through that door last spring. Ned Clayburn dozed behind the desk. Through the archway he could see the fat bartender and a couple of gamblers looking down on their luck. He asked the number of Dad's room and climbed the stairs.

Dad answered his knock almost instantly, blinking for a second before seeing who it was. 'Oh, it's you, Joe.' He wore trousers, undershirt, and wool socks. The bristly stand of his gray hair showed that he had just got out of bed. He scratched at his whiskers and said, 'I was just standing here figuring whether I ought to get shaved at the barber's or save two bits and pull 'em out myself.'

He was curious about Joe's visit, but he asked no questions. He let Joe come inside, close the door, and make the first query.

Joe asked, 'What you going to do about all that killing down along the badlands?'

Dad, still scratching his whiskers, said: 'In this country a rustler caught in the act is fair game to anybody able to kill him. I'm an old-fashioned man and I don't tamper with custom.'

'I'm not talking about what happened at Art Gamey's. I'm talking about what they did to Stellingworth.'

Dad fastened him with narrowed pale eyes. '*What* did they do to Stellingworth?'

'You mean you didn't hear? They killed him and burned him in his own cabin. And they didn't stop there. They burned out the homesteaders along the Goosebill and out the other way, along Dixon Creek.'

'*Who* did it?'

'North, that's who.'

'Joe, it's one thing to *think* somebody's responsible and another thing to know it. You know they got burned out, and you think North did it—isn't that right?'

'I tell you I *know* it was North. Him and Garfield and that bunch. Eaton had the rest down in the badlands or someplace. I saw 'em leave Stellingworth's when the fire was still going. They weren't any farther away than from here to the middle of the street. Heard 'em talking. That's how I knew they'd killed Stellingworth even before Jake Stroop and the others dug his body out of the ashes.'

Dad reached and dug his bony fingers into Joe's shoulder. 'Joe, have I got your word as a Wolverton that you're giving me the straight honest truth?'

'Yes!'

'Could you identify everybody with him?'

'Half of 'em, I could. There was Garfield and Red Tripplett and Dick Dean—'

'Not too loud!' He opened the door and looked both ways along the hall. 'You'll have to keep quiet about this. That's a tough bunch. They wouldn't shy at killing you if they thought you could testify against them. Now tell me everything you know.'

In telling his story Joe left out all mention of his visit to Gamey's or of bringing Holly out, but he told of their attack on the ranch and the things he'd learned at Newhall's. He finished by saying: 'If you ask me, North's getting ready to take over this country. He's damn' near—'

'No, he hasn't and he's not going to. Where's Holly now?'

'He left the country.'

'Ma at the ranch alone?'

'Just her and old Hap.'

'All right. You better go back and stay with her. Sit tight and take care of your own affairs. Don't go around looking for trouble. I'll do that. I'm paid for it.' He laughed and scratched at his whiskers. 'I can't afford a two-bit shave at a barbershop, but I'm paid for it.'

*   *   *

Dad had his shave at the barbershop after all. Joe's bronc was gone when he came outside. He crossed to the jail and found Wasey Slager playing two-handed pitch across the corner of the desk with John Temple, editor of the weekly paper.

'That kid leave town?' Dad asked.

Slager nodded. Mention of Joe brought color to his cheeks. 'He's looking for trouble, and one of these days he's going to look too

206

hard and find more of it than he can handle. He'll get himself killed, and then they'll expect the sheriff's office to do something about it.'

'That might happen. I'll tell you something else that might happen. He might go out and kill somebody, and then we'd have a worse job on our hands. Dude Gallagher saw the kid shoot one time and swears he's better than Holly. Not so fast, but better. That's pretty good shooting, when you're better than Holly.'

Slager gave him a quick glance and slammed down the last two cards in his hand, saying, 'Jack and the game!' He pocketed the quarter Temple tossed to him. 'Tell him to tie into Garfield. There's some opposition for him.'

'I don't want him tying into anybody.' Dad waited until Temple was gone before asking, 'Was he here talking to you?'

'Yes.'

'What'd he say?'

'Just that Stellingworth had been killed. He wanted to see you. I knew you wanted some sleep and tried to steer him out of town—'

'Did he tell you who killed Stellingworth?'

'No. Did he tell you?'

Dad said No and let the subject drop. In the morning he saddled his big gray horse and rode out the west road, through a gap of the Coalbanks, reaching the Snaky G home ranch when evening started to turn purple in the foothill valleys.

Ned Garfield saw him and walked up from one of the log bunkhouses. 'You better come down to the cookhouse for supper,' he said. 'Cray's not here, and what that China cook fixes when he's by himself I wouldn't know, except that it's getting so you can't find a skunk within two miles.'

After remarking that he'd eaten mountain possum one time, Dad managed to light his burned-out cigarette without burning his mustache in the process. 'Where *is* Cray?'

Garfield laughed in a quiet manner that gave his answer, 'Gone to Musselshell,' a special significance.

'Notice he most always takes you boys along except when he goes to Musselshell.'

'For that business he's got in Musselshell, he says he don't need our help.'

'Why doesn't he marry her and bring her home?'

'She's already got a man.'

They were talking about Ruby Tolliver, who had deserted her husband in Fort Benton and had gone in partnership with a gambler, known as the Duke of Orleans, to operate a place in Musselshell Landing.

Dad slept in a spare room of the ranch house and spent most of the following day sitting in the awning's shade. He was there, puffing a cigarette under his smoke-tanned mustache, when Creighton North got back. North nodded as though there was nothing the least unusual about finding the sheriff waiting for him. He pumped water from the rain cistern and, stripped to the belt, proceeded to lather and scrub himself.

'It's come to my notice,' Dad said, 'that you been getting pretty rough with those settlers down on Goosebill.'

North, without turning, said: 'You got your men mixed, haven't you? It's Major Eaton that is interested in Goosebill.'

'There was some burnings along Dixon Creek, too. That's on the range your outfit claims.'

'What is this, Sheriff, an arrest?'

'You killed Stellingworth and burned his place—ain't that the truth?'

North spun around and barked, 'No!' Then, getting control of himself: 'Who told you it was me that burned Stellingworth?'

'That's neither here nor there.'

North used the towel, gave it a hard twirl down across the roller, and said: 'I'm not one to make apologies for killing a rustler, so don't get the idea I'm losing my guts when I say that I didn't have anything to do with it. But just for the sake of discussion, say I *did* do it, what then?'

'Then, Cray, I'd have to take you in.'

'For getting rid of a *rustler* you'd take me in?'

'I heard Stellingworth was a rustler. I heard that Guffy and Newhall were rustlers. I even

209

heard you were a rustler. Hang all the men in Grant County accused of rustling, and all you'd have left would be two old maids and a Chinaman. And I'm not too sure about one of the old maids. Mind you, I'm not kicking up any racket about your trip to Gamey's. That's over the rim of the badlands and beyond my jurisdiction; I made that clear when I took the office. But homesteaders are something else. Lots of them have title to their land under the Veterans' Act.'

'This is a cattle country and it's staying a cattle country.'

'There's considerable talk about you and Major Eaton splitting the country up between you. You haven't listened to that talk so long you think maybe it's true?'

'You know as well as I do we're only two votes in the Association.'

'The Association's not running the country, either, Cray.'

'That's what you really rode out here to tell me?'

'I could have told you that in town. I rode out here to say there hadn't better be any more Stellingworths.'

Dad Tripp left when supper was over. As soon as he was up the first pitch of the trail, North walked to the mess house and called Garfield off the bench where he was listening to Jack Petit sing camp-meeting songs to the accompaniment of his fiddle.

North said, 'He's raising hell about Stellingworth.'

At first Garfield was incredulous. 'What could *he* do?'

'He's an ornery old fool. It's hard to tell what he would do if he got his back up. I wouldn't want the Major to hear the truth of it.'

Garfield looked up the road where Tripp was still visible in the late twilight. 'Oh, the hell with him. He can't prove anything.'

'Dad's not a bluffer. I think he does know it was us that put the scorch on Stellingworth. He practically told me he had a witness. We better drift in to town. Slag could tell us who it is.'

The smile had left Garfield's lips, and he said in his quiet, Southern voice, 'Y'all know where this will end up, don't you?'

'That isn't the point.'

'With me, seh, it is.' Garfield, a ne'er-do-well, was the product of a Texas plantation home, and his roots revealed themselves in the deft politeness of his tongue at times like these. 'It'll end by being one of those half-grown kids of Newhall's.'

North's lips curled down and he said, 'What if it is?'

'Why, just like I told you, I'm havin' no part in gunnin' down any kids.'

'You know what the Major would do if he found out it was us that burned out those

211

nesters? He's scared yellow for fear the Interior Department will send the soldiers in. Why, he'd carve us right out of the Association. You're in this as deep as I am, and you'll get yourself out of it the same way.'

'Why, seh, I would call that a matter for speculation.'

The antagonism that had long smoldered between them seemed about to flame into the open. Then North checked himself and said: 'Sleep on it. Anyhow, we're probably just borrowing trouble.'

Garfield, in his velvet voice, said, 'Why, that's the worst kind.'

On arriving back at the ranch, Joe again questioned Ma about Holly, about his wound, about his destination, and whether or not he got through the Association men.

'I told you he did, didn't I?' Ma said, her back turned, sounding short-tempered.

'He must have given you some idea where he'd head for.'

'He was going any direction he figured he could get away.'

'Didn't he say he'd be back?'

'He didn't say anything.'

Early next morning Joe saddled and rode to the line shack. He knew Holly wouldn't be there, but the place drew him; they had met there so often in the past.

The next morning, after cooking a supply of hard dummy, he rode across the Coalbanks and down the coulee to the badlands, to Pete Fontaine's, where he waited, with the dogs baying at him, until the old wolfer finally decided it was safe and showed himself.

'They hang nine, ten men, you savvy? I theenk maybe they come here, try to hang me. They kill Holly, no?'

'No. He was shot up and got away. I thought maybe he came here.'

'I don' see heem.'

'How about Chad Newhall?'

'He get away across *rivière*.'

That was good news. Joe was tempted to ride straight back and tell Jennie. Instead he asked directions to Gamey's and kept going.

Somewhere along the way he took a wrong turn and ended on the Missouri. It was noon of the next day when he found Gamey's. The valley was deserted, as he knew it would be. Turning back, he followed a ridge out to the line shack and reached Newhall's at midnight.

Jennie sat down and wept when she heard that her husband was safely across the river.

Joe said, 'I didn't hear anything about Holly.'

She checked her crying and looked up. 'Joe—you sure Holly got away?'

He felt sick. 'Course I am! Ma said he did. Why, what'd you hear?'

'Nothing. I shouldn't have said anything. Only Tommy said he didn't get away that night.'

'You mean they caught him before he got to the breaks?'

'He never got away at all. That's what Tommy heard. He's got a friend, a breed kid that wrangles horses for Goosebill. Of course, there's probably no truth to it. You can't believe a breed.'

'Ma said he got clear.'

'Then he did. And don't look at me like that. I been praying he'd got away. Next to my own man, I hoped *he'd* get away!'

He made a bed on the floor and tried to sleep, but nightmare figures kept crossing his mind. Without waiting for breakfast, he rode to the home ranch where he found Ma sitting on an upended bucket outside the shed, splicing harness. She didn't pause in her work, but he could sense how relieved she was to see him.

'Joe, where you been?'

'Around.' He made an indefinite motion toward the badlands. 'I was hoping to run across Holly.' He waited for her to say something. 'Are you dead sure he got away that night?'

'What's the matter with you, anyhow? How many times do I have to answer that question? Yes, he got away! Now I wish you'd quit prowling the country, trying to run into trouble.'

He didn't repeat what Jennie Newhall had told him. It would only make Ma dislike her more than she did already.

He let down the gate bar to take his horse in the corral. Something made him glance around. Old Hap was peering at him from one of the shed windows. He'd been eavesdropping.

Joe was about to say something in anger, but he checked himself when Hap laid a finger at his lips in a sign of secrecy. He pulled the saddle off his horse and carried it inside the shed.

'What d'you want?'

'You come along,' Hap whispered. 'There's something I think you ought to see.'

He was led across the creek and deep into a chokecherry bramble. There Hap hunted beneath some logs and drew out a revolver. It was a forty-five-caliber Colt with some scars along the trigger guard that identified it as Holly's.

Joe took it from him. 'Where'd you get this?'

'Found it down in the old garden plot.'

Trying to fight down his fear, Joe said, 'Holly probably lost it when he made his run.'

'Ma's been looking for this. I see her down there searching the ground every day when you're not around. Back and forth, back and forth, just hunting the ground. That's why I sneaked over and had a look, too. Somebody'd stepped on it and shoved it down in that soft dirt.' He saw Joe start away with the gun and grabbed him. 'Don't let Ma know I showed it to you. If you say anything, say you found it yourself.'

He thought and said, 'I won't say anything.'

He put the gun in the band of his pants and pulled his shirt over it. He ate breakfast, and after Ma drove up the creek with a load of stock salt he went down to the old garden patch and looked around. Each scene of the fight kept passing his mind's eye. He kept thinking of Ellen Eaton, how she'd come to him in the shed, how she'd kept him there with tears and pleading and even physical strength. Ma had told her to keep him there. Growing in him was an awful fear as to *why* she'd kept him there.

He saddled a long-legged buckskin and rode to the Goosebill, waiting until late twilight before he dropped down to the creek. He left his horse deep in the brush, took off his spurs, and walked up a creek trail to the upper corrals.

It was dark now. A lantern burned in the blacksmith shop where someone was hammering on metal. When the hammering stopped and the loud dissonance faded in his ears, he could hear, sharp and pure on the cool air, the chording of a guitar and a voice singing verse after verse in Spanish, each ending, '. . . *serà por el amor de Dios.*'

He made a circle that took him to the rear of the house. He had brief glimpses of lighted windows through the straight rows of cottonwoods as he walked down and climbed the rail fence.

He was barely out of sight when a horseman, holding a rifle across the pommel of his saddle, rode out of the darkness and skirted the fence. Joe thought for a second that he had been seen, and his hand closed on the sharp-etched stock of his forty-five, but the horseman barely paused, and rode on. In four or five minutes he was back again. A sentry, and through luck, Joe had slipped past. He should have known that Eaton, an army man, would have sentries out after that trouble in the badlands.

He moved forward through the trees and stopped when a scant dozen steps of open ground separated him from the house. The lighted windows were on the north side. He considered going around for a peep inside, but he waited; and after a timeless interval, while the moon rose, he had the impression of light shifting inside the house. Someone was carrying a lamp along an upstairs corridor. The light became bright in a window at the south corner, and moving quickly around, he had a glimpse of Ellen's silhouette. The window was open and he spoke her name. She had been moving but now she stopped. The light went out. It was too dark to see her, but he knew she was close to the window, peering down.

She said, sounding short of breath, 'Who is it?'

'Joe.'

'Wait there!'

He was hidden by a clump of lilac bushes. He didn't want her to find him skulking, and when she got down he had moved out into the open.

'Joe!' she whispered, coming close. 'Joe, you shouldn't have!' It put him off balance, having her near, and for a few seconds he forgot the reason for his coming.

She said: 'Dad would kill you if he caught you here. He would, Joe! You don't know him—his awful temper. He knows I was at the ranch that night. That night of the fight. He told me he'd kill you if he ever caught us together.'

Mention of the fight brought him back to his purpose. 'I had to see you. About Holly.'

'Oh, Joe!'

Her tone took him back to that night in the shed. She was ready to cry again. Suddenly Joe knew, without asking, that Holly was dead. He knew, without asking, that Ellen had known it that night. She had kept him away so that Ma could bury him.

He said in a tired voice, 'Holly's dead, isn't he?'

Her whisper was barely audible. 'Yes.'

He felt sick and empty. He had suspected it all along, but until now hope and fear would not let him admit it.

She whispered: 'She didn't want you to find out. She was afraid you'd go looking for North.'

'It was North that killed him!' He seized her hard by the arms, sinking fingers into her soft flesh until she clenched her teeth and caught her breath in pain. 'He did, didn't he? Or was it your dad who did it?'

'No, it wasn't Dad! He might have wanted him dead, but just the same he'd have taken him in for a jury trial. He never wanted to attack anybody except Gamey's outfit. From the start he's been scared of getting everybody lined up against the big outfits. I know he threatened to kill Holly on account of me, but he wouldn't use that way of doing it. He wouldn't pick on him when he was wounded. I know how you hate my Dad, and you know how I feel about him, too—'

'It was North!' he said through his teeth.

'Yes.'

'He found Holly and shot him without giving him a chance.'

She was trying to twist away. 'Let me go. Please, you're hurting me.'

He let go and she stepped back, rubbing her bruised arms. She saw him turn to leave and said: 'Joe, don't let Ma know I told you. She didn't want you to find out.'

'That's what she was doing while you were with me in the shed: she was making a deal with North not to tell about Holly if they didn't.'

'She was burying him.'

'Where'd she bury him?'

'Inside the old cabin. It was awful for her, Joe. She did it for you. She didn't want you to go out and get killed. You're all she's got left.'

'I ain't blaming her. I won't say anything. I ain't even going over there.'

'Where *are* you going?'

'I'm going to find North.'

She got hold of him as she had at the hotel and at the shed, but then he had wanted her to win. Tonight there was nothing like that in the back of his mind. With a firm thrust he pushed her away. Without looking back, he strode straight across the yard and around corrals and brush to where his buckskin waited.

CHAPTER THIRTEEN

Reaching the stage road, he headed toward Box Elder. If North wasn't in town, he'd probably find him at the ranch. He'd find him somewhere. He'd keep riding until he found him.

He pushed the buckskin hard, letting up only when his excitement had burned off. Toward morning, with fatigue making his body numb, he crossed to the springs on Toston Coulee, picketed his horse, and slept beneath the scant protection of a saddle blanket through the last chill hours, until the sun grew hot. Then he went on, not suspecting that Ellen Eaton, stealing away from the ranch after her father had retired, had passed him less than an hour before.

On reaching Box Elder, Ellen noticed that three horses wearing the Great Western iron were tied in front of the Bonanza Bar. The thought of North being in town gave her a sudden fright. She didn't know what color horse Joe was riding, but there were only two others in sight and neither had the Wolverton brand. Perhaps, she thought, he'd gone home after all.

People were looking at her, and she hated to be seen going to the jail office. By luck she found Dad Tripp seated on the hotel porch, looking at a frayed copy of the *Butte Miner.*

She told him about Joe and he got up quickly, saying: 'You did right in coming to me. I'll keep my eye out.' He stopped on his way down the steps and turned to ask, 'Your daddy know where you are?'

'No.'

'Well, you know him as well as I do. You better go over to Sisty's and wait there.'

From the front window of Sisty Dehon's Millinery and Ready-made Shop, she watched Dad walk the length of the main street, looking in each place as he passed. Sisty, a large, motherly-looking spinster, talked

221

steadily, showing her a number of new bonnets just in from St. Louis. She then prepared tea, and Ellen sat down with her, uncomfortably, rising each minute or two to glance from the window.

'What's wrong with you, Ellen?' Sisty asked.

'I'll be back!' Ellen had glimpsed Joe Wolverton just as he crossed the bridge of Box Elder Creek a quarter-mile from town. 'I have to see Dad Tripp.'

She started across to the jail office. Trying to walk, she ran in spite of herself. Men drifting toward the stage station for the Tuesday mail delivery stopped to watch as she ran, light-footed as a deer, with her riding skirt switching behind her.

She stopped in the office door, seeing not Dad Tripp, as she'd expected, but Wasey Slager.

'Where's Dad?'

'He's at the barbershop.' Slager followed as she backed to the sidewalk. 'Something I can do for you, Miss Eaton?'

'No!'

The barber had seen her and said something, and Dad, climbing from the chair, stood in the door and wiped lather from his half-shaved face.

She ran to him and cried, 'Dad, Joe's coming. He just crossed the bridge.'

'All right. You get back to Sisty's and don't worry.' He saw Sisty standing in the door with her eyes shaded and called, 'Miss Dehon, will you get her inside and see that she stays there?'

Dad ignored the questions fired at him, and with his long gangling stride covered the ground to the Bonanza. He found North at a card table in the rear, one boot on a chair, watching while a gambler nicknamed Highpockets fired a pair of dice repeatedly across the dirty green cloth, calling for a point. At the bar, drinking beer, were Ned Garfield and Dick Dean.

Dad stopped and said, 'Cray, could I speak to you for a minute?'

'Sure.' North watched one more pass of the dice, then letting his $5 gold piece lie, walked over in his stud-legged manner.

Dad said, 'Joe Wolverton's in town and I have an idea he's looking for trouble.'

North's eyes narrowed. 'You mean he's looking for me?'

'Yes, he's looking for you.'

'Thanks for warning me. I'll see that I don't get it in the back.'

'You won't get it in the back. I'm running this town, and there'll be no shooting at all if I can prevent it. You stay inside the Bonanza until I tell you to come out. And keep your men in here, too!'

Dean started to say something, but Garfield quieted him. North, lean and rocky-jawed, met the sheriff's gaze. 'You're going to shove me too far one of these days.'

'I'm not shoving you at all. It's for your protection as much as his. You ought to know that there's nothing in the world more dangerous than a crazy kid with a gun. Especially *this* crazy kid.'

North laughed with a jerk of his shoulders, saying, 'I'll be scared to stick my nose out all day.'

'You stay in here!' Dad's eyes were a little wild. 'Whenever the time comes I can't run this town, they can bury me.'

He went outside, down the street, waiting in front of the print shop until Joe took the shortcut from the stage road. He stepped down from the walk, then, and said, 'Hold it a minute!'

Joe reined in. His eyes, getting their first full look at the street, rested on the three saddlehorses tied in front of the Bonanza Bar. The Great Western used a G in a Circle as its horse brand, and he had no trouble in reading it at that distance.

Dad got him by one leg and asked, 'Where you headed?'

'Over town. What's wrong with that?'

'Nothing—unless you're here looking for trouble, and I know you are. You're looking for Cray North.'

'Where is he? At the Bonanza?'

'It makes no difference where he is; you're not seeing him.'

Joe tried to pull away, but Dad held on. He used the bit, and the buckskin, a rangy animal, came around, ramming Dad with his hindquarters so that he was almost pinned against the hitch rack. Dad got away by ducking beneath. He came up with his gun half drawn and fury whitening his face.

'Listen, you smart kid! There's not going to be any trouble between you and North. I'm still running this town!'

Joe checked the impulse to spur away. He said: 'I done nothing to be chased out of town. I'm hungry and I want to feed and water my horse.'

Dad held his temper and said: 'All right, go and do it. But stay away from the Bonanza. Stay away from that end of town.'

Joe rode down the street, past the Bonanza. He didn't turn. He merely watched from the corner of his eye. A bartender in a white apron was standing just behind the batwing doors. Beyond him lay a deeply shadowed interior. Men were in other doorways along the street, all watching him. It gave him a strange, almost giddy sensation, like an unsure actor making a first-act entrance. Passing the express office, he heard Soldier Jim's magpie voice: 'There's Joey Wolverton, and it's his night to howl.'

He didn't feel like laughing, but he did, swinging around slack in the saddle with one knee bent and his right hand on the cantle. Several others spoke to him, and he spoke back. He'd been noticing a difference in the way people treated him. Not like a kid any more. It was almost the same way they'd acted toward Holly when he rode back from that cattle-war country in Wyoming with a gunman's reputation tagging him.

He dismounted at the Apex Stable and turned the bridle over to Jake Kroop's hulking, feeble-minded son. Joe handed him a four-bit tip, the way he'd seen Holly do, saying, 'Give him the best.'

Before returning, he took off his shirt, pumped water over his back and shoulders, and dried himself with handfuls of hay. He thought it would take fever and excitement out of him, but it didn't. There was no room in his mind for anything except Creighton North— the hate and fear of him wound inseparably together.

He walked down the knoll, keeping watch on the Bonanza. Ellen came from Sisty's and called his name.

'You followed me!' he said.

'Yes, Joe. I had to . . .'

He didn't pay attention to what she was saying. He was thinking that Major Eaton would miss her at breakfast and start out after her.

'Your dad will be along. You better—'

'I don't care about my dad! I don't care what he says or what he tries to do. I'm never going back there again.' She'd come up beside him. She had hold of his arm, was pressing it against her side. Apparently she was afraid he'd pull away from her and go on down the street to find North. Her voice had become pleading: 'Joe, I left without a cent. I'm awfully hungry. I think they'll fix us a snack in the hotel.'

She led him around to the porch entrance of the dining room. It was empty, brilliantly sunlit, filled with the slightly sour steam-and-onion odor of frontier dining rooms everywhere.

A large woman with a flushed face saw them and came from the kitchen. She said that while it was still too early for dinner, she'd fry them something special. The something 'special' proved to be a huge meal of bacon, hotcakes, and stewed dry peaches.

After forcing down the first bite, Joe became ravenous. He forgot about everything until he had reached the peaches. Then he said: 'You can't just stay here in town. Your dad will be in before the day's over.'

'I'm leaving on the stage. It's almost time.'

'That's the northbound.'

'I know it. I'll go to Milk River and from there over to Benton. My mother had relatives in Benton.'

'You're not going back to *them.*'

'Yes, I am! And maybe they'll tell me where my mother is. I don't believe what dad says-that she just left without wanting me. I don't believe that! I think he drove her away.'

He glanced back at the kitchen. The woman was standing still just inside, listening. He dropped his voice. 'How can you? You haven't got enough money to get there.' Without pausing to wait for her reply, he slid the $20 gold piece that Holly had given him beneath the rim of her plate.

Ellen said, 'No,' but when he wouldn't take it back she slipped it in the pocket of her riding skirt.

Joe said, 'It's due at eleven.'

Outside, from the elevation of the front porch, they could see the south road rising in a dusty white line beyond the roofs. The stage was visible on it, its movements frozen by distance. It was the big Concord this time, and there was a six-horse team pulling it.

She said, 'I'll go down and buy my ticket.'

'Have you any luggage?'

'No.'

Stiff-spined, with his eyes straight ahead, Major Eaton was at that moment riding down the street on his big Kentucky gelding, with Alf Koenig on a half-blooded horse slightly behind. On coming around the express office platform, Eaton saw his daughter and Joe Wolverton hurrying down the plank walk. He had a braided quirt looped around his wrist. He cut with it, drove in his spurs, and the horse lunged directly at them.

Several men shouted a warning. Ellen, on

the inside, was somewhat out of danger, but Joe remained in the animal's path. He heard Ellen's scream and the warning shouts of men. He did a dive and roll, trying to get out of the way, but it was too late, and Eaton rode over him. The hoofs missed. Wheeling, Eaton tried to repeat, but the animal balked. He sprang to the ground and jerked the army colt from its holster high on his waist.

Joe was down with one arm bent over his head. His gun was pinned under him. Instead of trying to draw, he dived to partial protection beyond the edge of the sidewalk.

Ellen in the meantime had grabbed her father's arm. He twisted himself away. When she tried again, he struck her backhand, across the neck, knocking her to the ground. The sight brought Joe to his feet.

Eaton was holding his gun at his side. His head was up and his spine straight as a rifle barrel. He cried, 'You have a gun on you; I'm giving you your chance to draw it!'

Joe had taken a couple of steps backward. He knew that Eaton would get in the first shot and that he had to make that shot miss. He took another step, dived sidewise to the left, drawing as he went down.

Eaton recognized the maneuver and tried to lead him. The bullet was aimed too far. It struck the ground and drove dirt into Joe's face. He felt the sting of the dirt pellets mixed with the kick and explosion of his own gun.

Instinctively, he knew his bullet had gone home.

Eaton was knocked backward. Joe glimpsed him in a sitting position, legs folded under him, a baffled look in his eyes. Joe tried to check his second shot and couldn't, but he dropped his elbow and the bullet flew high. He rolled to his feet, realizing that Koenig, still on horseback, was behind him, just coming up with a gun. He could have killed Koenig, but he had no will to do it. He placed himself so that Koenig couldn't shoot because Eaton was in the line of fire, and ran for the partial cover of one of the hotel cottonwoods.

Koenig shot at him, but it was difficult range and his horse was fighting the bridle. The bullet cut leaves from a tree twenty feet to one side. The horse sunfished, dumped Koenig to the ground, and bucked away. Joe saw all that as he ran through the hotel yard, behind a Chinese washee, to the livery stable. The Kroop kid had watched the shooting and was staring at him with scared eyes.

'Get my horse,' Joe said.

He was surprised at the sound of his own voice. It gave no indication of how he felt. He might have been a Ned Garfield with uncounted gunfights behind him.

CHAPTER FOURTEEN

On a cutbank rim overlooking upper Gros Ventre Greek, Joe Wolverton sat through the hours of evening and twilight. A night wind flowed down from the Coalbanks, and suddenly he was so cold his teeth chattered. It was like waking up. He took an interest in being alive, and for the first time since leaving Box Elder the thought of pursuit made him nervous. He found the buckskin grazing belly-deep in grass along the creek bottom, mounted, and started to ride.

Exercise took the chill out of his body and put a new edge to his hunger. He thought of going to Ma's, but that would be the first place they'd look for him. Newhall's would be a better bet. It was close to morning when he got there.

Chad was home, and they shook hands. 'I heard about Holly,' he said, wanting to save Joe the pain of repeating it. 'What's happened now?'

'I just killed Major Eaton.'

Chad stared at him.

'Yeah, I killed him. He was slapping Ellen around. He drew first, and I—'

'Where was it? Over at your place?'

'It was in town.'

'And you made a run for it?'

'Yeah.'

'They'll have everybody in the country after you. I'll give you my dun horse and some grub. Stay clear of Gamey's and all the main crossings. You can get over the river any place now. Ever been in the Little Rockies?'

'I'm not leaving the country. I still got a score to settle.'

'Stay away from North! With his backing, it'd be suicide. Head for the Little Rockies. When you get there, ask how to reach Spotted Wolf Gulch. Look up a fellow named Three Finger Joe. Tell him who you are and why you're on the lope. Nobody'll bother you there. Lay around till things cool off, then drift on to the Milk River country or Canada. But stay clear of the army posts and stay clear of Benton.'

If he left the country, he'd never get guts enough to come back. Joe knew that as he rode toward the river. He had no intention of crossing over. It was just that he had no plan, nowhere to go.

The day had started out to be sunshiny. At the river it was overcast with an occasional misty sprinkle of rain. He built a fire, fried bacon and pan bread, brewed a pot of strong coffee. Eating gave him a feeling of confidence, so he turned back, and for want of a better place, ended at the line shack.

It was night, and so dark he could scarcely make out the summits of the Coalbanks. He was almost upon the cabin before he could see it. A natural wariness made him swing his horse away and ride to the creek. There he dismounted, climbed the corral, and walked across the pounded dry dirt. No fresh manure. He stopped at the woodpile. The ax was in its old place. He decided it was safe enough. Nobody would look for him there.

He walked on to the cabin. The plank door was shut. He had to lift and shove hard to open it. His momentum carried him inside, where the odor of fresh gun solvent struck his nostrils.

'Stand where you are!' a voice said from the blackness.

He checked the impulse to draw. Thrusting the door had put him out of position. He was helpless, silhouetted against the night light outside.

'What d'you want?' he cried.

'Just wanted to pass the time.'

It was the easy, half-amused drawl of Ned Garfield.

'Just take it easy,' Garfield said. 'I'm not going to kill you. I could have done that five minutes ago.'

It was then that Joe realized how scared he'd been. He held the door so that his legs wouldn't give out under him. He finally got a breath in his lungs and felt strong enough to walk.

Garfield struck a match. The flare was

unexpected, blinding after the long darkness. He lighted the bacon-grease dip, after the gunman's habit, with his left hand, leaving his right free.

'You better close the door, Joe.' He saw the burlap that Holly had used to curtain the window, and stretched it across. 'I sort of figured you'd be along. I been waiting all day. Wanted to tell you how hard North's looking to find you.'

'You mean on account of Major Eaton?'

'Hell, no. If the Major dies of that slug he took, North would celebrate for a week.'

Joe jerked suddenly erect. 'You mean the Major isn't dead?'

'Oh, you thought you'd killed him? No, he isn't dead. Not when I left, anyhow, and I doubt that he will. If he had been two hundred pounds of muscle and sinew, he'd have given up the spirit like that—' He blew out the match. 'It's those wiry fellows that die hard.'

Joe felt the flood of relief. He felt like someone long imprisoned in a hot, airless room who suddenly finds freedom in the open air. He hadn't realized, until then, how the killing of Ellen's father had weighed on him.

Garfield must have sensed that, for he said, 'You haven't too much to be happy about, kid. I meant that about North being out to get you. He's out to kill you any way he can.'

Joe knew that North hated him, but he hadn't expected to be marked for bushwhack,

234

at least ahead of Newhall and all the others.

'Why am I so important? He's got the best part of our range.'

'Because you were an eyewitness that night at Stellingworth's, and Stellingworth owned his land under the Veterans' Act, and somebody wrote some letters and got the G.A.R. stirred up over in Helena. There'll be investigators in from the Interior Department. He don't want 'em getting any signed statements. You know, Joe, you're a pretty big man in North's life right now.'

'The Association will stand behind him, and they always ran Grant County to suit—'

'The Association will throw him to the wolves. They never backed him in raiding the homesteaders. He did that on his own. He thought that once the fight got hot there was no way the others could back out; he misjudged on that. Now, with the G.A.R. raising hell, Tom Nenus and the Major, neither one, will admit a speaking acquaintance with him. Of course, if it weren't for you, nobody could prove anything. You see now why he has every man on his payroll out gunning for you?'

'Who let him know I was at Stellingworth's? Was it Dad?'

'It was Wasey Slager.' Garfield watched him without appearing to, and in the casually deft way he did everything, rolled a cigarette. 'It's sure nice up in that Milk River country this time o' yeah,' he said, with an exaggeration of his usual Southwestern drawl.

'He ain't running me out of the country.'

'Why, that may be, but one false step and you'll never *get* out of the country. They're out to plant you, kid. I been traveling with bad companions over at the Snaky G. Tripplett's all right, but most of 'em won't hesitate to carve a cold-meat notch. Not when there's $500 in it for 'em. You better consider and go north with me till things quiet down. Fellow by the name of Jim Hill's building a railroad up there, and we'll find money that'll beat cowboying.'

Joe said, 'He killed Holly.' Then he asked with sudden doubt, 'Well, he did, didn't he?'

'Yes, he did.' Garfield no longer tried to argue him out of staying. Inhaling to the last cubic inch of his lungs, he sat back and talked smoke from his mouth. 'Better tell you where the boys are. Might change by tomorrow, but this'll help. Jerome and the Tookas Kid are watching your home ranch. Red Tripplett's at the cable ferry. He's got a man at Wing Coulee and one at Thirty Mile—'

'I was just at Thirty Mile.'

'You were lucky. Don't try it again. Don't go anywhere again where you ever went before. There's a new man, calls himself Powder River Johnny, at Box Elder. Dick Dean and Cowan are watching the trail to Musselshell. Wargo is at Lodge Grass stage station in case you

236

headed out toward Miles. He's even got men across the river on the roads to Little Rocky and Crow Butte. I asked to watch these lower Coalbanks because I was sure as anything you'd come here.'

'How come *you* didn't kill me?'

'I don't know. I never was one to figure why I did this thing or why I did that. I do what I feel like. I guess I'm what you'd call a natural man. Now, you repeat all those places I told you.'

Joe did, and Garfield said, 'He's got a few more roving around, just for luck.'

'Who they going to collect that $500 from if North isn't around to pay it?'

Garfield smiled in his slow manner, saying: 'Why, seh, that strikes at the heart of the matter. Trouble is, North isn't a great hand to show himself alone. That was one of my jobs, up until today, seeing he had a little bit of an edge over anybody that wanted to tangle with him. But there is one place he likes to go all by himself. To Musselshell. He has a girl there by the name of Ruby Tolliver. She helps run a place called the—'

'I know who she is. Is he in Musselshell now?'

'It's a good bet. You see, by North's book you should be a dead man by tomorrow, and he'd like to be far off, with witnesses. But sit around, look the town over to make sure. He might have taken Dick Dean with him, this once.'

That's what Garfield had come for, to tell him where to find North alone, and now that it was done, he stood and stretched himself.

'You hungry, Joe? Let's fix a bite, and I'll drift a ways with you. It's too stuffy for sleepin' indoors.'

They rode together through a cold sprinkle of rain toward the crest of the Coalbanks, following no trail.

'Men are peculiar animals,' Garfield was saying. 'Take Cray, now. You know, he'd give up his last dollar and share his pants right down the middle for a man that'd tell him, 'Cray, you're the boss.' He's a ridge runner. He wants to boss the herd. You can tell that in the way he carries himself on those percheron legs of his. That's why he'd rather boss a big outfit like the Snaky G than own a small place of his own that'd pay him three times as much money. You want to think of that when you go lookin' for him, Joe.'

'Why?'

'Because if he thinks you're scared, nothing can stop him. Some men are like one o' them Chihuahua oranges. Crack through that hard peeling, and the inside runs between your fingers. Cray never told me about his boyhood, but I happen to know he comes from shanty folk in the Mississippi bottoms south of St. Louis who were so busted even the Negroes kicked 'em around. I suppose he swore if he

ever climbed up from that shack he'd do some bossing on his own, and he sure has. He's convinced himself that he's the real lobo leading the pack. It ain't just North like that. A man's whatever he thinks he is. Why, I recall an old fellow down in Maverly who thought he was Stonewall Jackson. He used to go around in one o' them old-time gray Confederate capes and shout cavalry orders. Some of the cowboys up from Texas had been cavalrymen and they used to execute 'em just for the hell of it; and it was a sight to see, them drunk and him crazy. Well, he died in the mountain-fever epidemic of '85, and the boys decided to buy a monument for his grave with 'Stonewall Jackson' carved on it and they went around collecting money. There, in town at that time, was a harness maker, a Yankee who'd been corporal under Stoneman and lost one eye at Kelley's Ford, and he said he'd see us dead before he gave so much as a two-cent piece to build a monument over any damned Confederate general. You see, old Stonewall really believed it so hard he had that harness maker believing it, too.'

CHAPTER FIFTEEN

They parted at Squawhammer Creek, whe Ned Garfield turned toward the river. 'W

out for Dean and Cowan,' he called over his shoulder.

'And you look out for Gamey and McBride.'

'I'll look out for *Gamey*.'

It was the first intimation that Joe had that Muddy McBride had been killed.

He rode through misty rain, across pathless prairie country, down to Horsefly Creek, and up again. There he reached the freight road and, taking Garfield's advice, left it and dropped down on the rough country overlooking Musselshell River.

Daylight came through steady rain. His clothes were wet; his hat was a sodden cold lump on his head. Droplets, gathering along the brim, flowed to the front and grew larger until they fell. It got to be a game, trying to make them strike the saddle horn. Aching from the saddle, he reached a shack standing below a hoof-trampled spring.

He dismounted, drank from a cow track, and looked the place over. Apparently the shack had been unoccupied since last winter. The brand, Lazy M Quarter-circle, was burned in the arch log of the door. That was an outfit from still farther on, in the high land beyond the Musselshell.

He cooked the rest of his bacon on the little rusty stove, dried off his clothes, and laid down for a nap.

It was hard to guess time through the overcast, but when he awoke it seemed to be

midafternoon. He rode down the Musselshell. Darkness settled early. The rain, coming harder, beat on a denim jacket turned stiff and cold. At last he glimpsed the lights of Musselshell Landing sprinkled along a bench half a mile from the junction of the rivers.

The main street, placed above the reach of June floods, was a line of log and frame one-story fronts facing the Missouri. The town had come into existence as a trading post of the Upper Missouri Company a good fifteen years before Box Elder, and though the surveyors had included it in Grant County, it never admitted subservience to the younger town and was actually a law unto itself, which was to say it had no law at all except the standards of the frontier individually applied by means of a six shooter or, rarely, a mob and a hangman's rope.

But for all that the Landing was generally a quiet place, sleeping winter and summer by the great river, a town where old Indian fighters passed their last years sitting under the awnings in fine weather and in the heat of the Stevens Company's ornate pot-gutted stove when it was wet and cold.

Tonight there was no sign of anyone. He rode down the rain-slick street, watching the misted windows of log-shanty saloons. There was a two-story building farther up where the bench narrowed and a steep bank plunged toward the Missouri. That was the Palace

241

Theatre, the place run by Ruby Tolliver and the Duke of Orleans.

He drew up in front. The hitch rack was empty. Voices came through the claptrap walls, the voices of men and women, separated by areas of silence. He heard a door close and boots thudding along a plank walk.

He'd resolved to remain relaxed, but the thought that this man might be North made his muscles freeze. Then, against a lighted window, he saw that it was an undersized man toting a roll of Sugans on his shoulder. Joe felt ashamed and rode over.

The man, seeing him, drew up and said: 'Why, Holly—Oh, you ain't Holly.'

'I'm Joe Wolverton.'

'Sure, his kid brother.'

They'd never met before, but the man evidently thought they had for he didn't introduce himself. He stepped down from the sidewalk and dropped the Sugan roll so that it rested on his boot toe. He was at some ageless period of life between forty and seventy, with a face leathered by sun until it resembled the sole of an old moccasin.

Joe said, 'Is Cray North in town?'

'Why—' he thought for a while, 'why, yes, I'd say he was. Had a man with him, too. Dick Dean. They're at the Palace. Were, not five minutes ago. Did you look?'

Joe cursed through his teeth. North had always come to Musselshell alone, but *this* time he'd brought Dean.

The man said: 'He tooken a fancy to Ruby Tolliver, you know. Not that I blame him. I wish I was eighty again, I'd be swinging my rope for one of her hind feet, too.' He giggled and leaned over to spit tobacco juice.

'Where's she live?'

'Not there. She got a house out back. Right on lover's leap where the Gros Ventre maiden jumped to her death for the love of Liver-eatin' Johnson.' He jabbed at Joe's chap-encased leg significantly. 'Ruby ain't one of the girls, Joe. She's real class. St. Louis class. Why, when the sternwheelers are running in the spring there ain't a captain on the river that don't make it a point to tie here for twenty-four hours, and you *should see* the fancy-wine blowouts she puts on. Pours enough high-priced liquor to win an election in Helena. They drink the stuff out of a gal's slipper, too. Just like in the temperance lectures.'

Joe said good night to him and rode around to the back. There it was very dark. A walk of half-flat poles led through bottle heaps and sheds to a small, snug little house of squared logs on an exposed strata of sandrock with the steep slope of an eroded gumbo bank dropping toward the river on the far side. Behind the house stood a horse shelter consisting of a roof and wall to break the north wind.

The house was dark, apparently empty. He

listened, and heard the movements of a horse beneath the shelter. He rode over. There were two horses. It was too dark to read brands, but they were saddled, and the shine of some big silver rosette conchas identified one of the saddles as North's.

He dismounted, led his own horse out of sight behind the shed, and tied him. He walked back to the house. He listened for almost a minute this time. He still hadn't made up his mind what to do. He rapped, expecting no answer and getting none. Then he opened the door and stepped inside.

The strong odor of perfume struck his nostrils. The room was warm. After so many hours in the rainy freshness, it made him feel off balance. Fire glow came through the cracks of a cookstove. He groped toward it, lifted one of the lids with his jackknife, and by the ruddy light made out the main features of the house. There were two rooms joined by an arch—the kitchen he was standing in and a combined living room and bedroom. A leather-padded chair stood just beyond the arch, partly concealed by some drapes of strung beads. He closed the stove, walked to the chair, and sat down.

Excitement kept him on edge. His mind moved over a thousand thoughts without fastening on any of them. From the black silence a clock was ticking. It ticked louder and louder. He commenced to wonder if he'd be able to hear anyone coming, over the tick of the clock. He had entered the house on the impulse of the moment. Now he wondered if North would come there at all. The woman might come alone. If the two were together, he might be unable to shoot it out with North because of her. There were too many 'ifs.' But he waited. It was his only chance to meet North without Dean.

A door closed and he heard the thump of boots. He made an instinctive move for his gun. It might be rammed too tightly in the holster. He lifted it, dropped it very lightly. He wouldn't want it there too lightly, either, so that some quick movement would make it fall. He lifted it again, and his hand, suddenly out of control, jerked and let the gun drop. It struck his boot and clattered on the floor. He groped for it. It wasn't where he expected. Suddenly desperate, he sprang over and jerked a lid off the range. The gun lay two steps away. He picked it up and faced the door with it in his hand. He couldn't just wait with it drawn. That would be bushwhack. He returned it to the holster. The stove lid was still off. Perhaps North had stopped, taking alarm at the slight fire glow. He went to the door, opened it quickly, and quickly stepped outside.

There was nothing. The boots had been far away, on the platform walk in front. He went back, replaced the stove lid, sat in the chair.

He felt burned out. North, in his mind, was

still a power inevitable and destroying. North was going to kill him. Once he resigned himself to that, it was easier to wait. The clock—he could hear its ticking again. He passed the time by counting its ticks to a hundred, to a thousand, and then started over again. The rain, blown by gusts from the river, rattled like shot against the windowpanes. It stopped, leaving a rapid *drip-drip,* and he knew that a shake had been blown off the roof.

Then he heard the thud of a loose plank on the wall close outside. A scant second later the door opened. A woman was silhouetted against the dim glow of night. He sat straight, rigid, watching for North to appear behind her. He didn't. She was alone. She closed the door and her perfume struck him, stronger than before, but fresh, mixed with the smell of rain. She lifted the stove lid and an amber glow flooded her. He'd expected someone much younger. She was about thirty, tall and deep-breasted, her skin white, her hair almost black. Her beauty was striking; it had glitter, but it also had hardness.

She was lighting a splinter. It burst into flame and she carried it to the lamp. After adjusting the wick, she stripped off her black raincoat and shook out the long thick coils of her hair. Joe was in full view, and she was facing him, but he had not moved and nothing attracted her attention to him. She ran fingers through her hair, getting droplets of rain from

246

it; then, forking it back with her fingers, she walked to the window and tried to see outside.

He could hear someone stamping mud off 's boots. That would be North. He'd stopped 'eed his horse, and now he was ready to me in the door. The moment had at last rived, and suddenly all excitement flowed m Joe's body. He was himself again, except ior a slight tingling in his muscles. He had :arcely breathed since Ruby Tolliver had entered. Now he took a deep breath and stood up. She heard him and whirled around.

His hand was outspread, just below the butt of his Colt. Against his dark clothing the gun's nickel and mother-of-pearl gleamed brightly, and it stopped her in momentary indecision.

Then the door flew open and North came in.

He took one step and then, seeing Joe, drew up with a suddenness that reared his body backward.

Ruby Tolliver found her voice and cried, 'Cray!'

Surprise vanished from North's face, and something else crept into its place. His lips were parted, showing the bottom row of his teeth. Tendons stood out rigidly in his neck. His face, where the light struck it, was the color of dead ashes. His lips moved and no words came. His throat seemed to be constricted. At last he got the words out, 'What do you want?'

'You been looking for me, haven't you?' Joe had not known what he was going to say. The quality of his voice surprised him, too; it was so controlled and quiet.

North said, 'Would I be over *here* looking for you?'

The wavering edge of his voice cried the terror inside him. He had turned gutless. He looked sick to his stomach. He looked like one stricken with poison.

Joe's hatred of him, so long stored up and intensified by fear, turned to contempt. He said: 'No, *you* haven't been looking for me. You sneaked down here and left your gunmen to it.'

'I didn't! Joe, somebody's been filling you with lies. I got nothing more to settle with you. Any of our differences can be settled inside the Association.'

'Go for your gun!'

'Listen to me—'

'Go for your gun!'

North's hands were down, rigid, with his fingers stretched toward the floor. Every muscle of his body seemed to be rigid. Sweat glistened on his cheeks. His eyes shot over to the woman and back again.

The eyes were warning. Ruby Tolliver, turning, struck the lamp chimney with her forearm. It shattered on the floor and she blew out the flame.

As the chimney crashed, Joe saw Creighton

North's right hand swing up for the gun at his thigh.

The rest came without thinking. Joe drew with a slack turn of his body. The etched mother-of-pearl clung to his hand. The gun was like a part of him. It seemed to aim itself. It rocked in his hand. The room was ripped by flame and concussion. By the last glimmer of lamplight he saw North driven back against the door.

North had fired twice, perhaps three times. Bullet-shocked, he shot wild. A sliver stabbed Joe's cheek. He brushed it away and moved along the wall. The woman was on him, clawing with feline fury. Without looking, he backhanded her out of the way.

North was no longer in the door. Joe followed. He could see nothing. He started around the corner, and North's gun exploded, slicing a riffle through mud. Joe fired back at the powder flash. He kept going. He realized, more by sound than sight, that North was up and running. Stumbling, he had reached the horse shed. Somehow, wounded as he was, he got his horse untied and climbed to the saddle. Joe told himself he couldn't let him get away. He'd have to settle it tonight, yet he couldn't fire point-blank into his back.

He started up the sidewalk with the gun poised in his hand. The horse, running, had been turned too sharply and lost footing in the slippery gumbo. He fell and came up again with North unsaddled, one boot caught in the stirrup. The horse bolted, sunfishing. North's head and shoulders were on the ground. The terrified horse trampled him and dragged him.

North was still being dragged when Joe lost sight of them beyond the Palace. He kept running. Men were outside. They were gathered around North, who was left in a muddy heap just short of the hitching racks. They got out of Joe's way, suddenly silent when they saw the gun in his hand. North's head was bent under him in a disjointed manner. It reminded him of the men who had been left hanging at Gamey's.

'Neck broken,' one of them said. 'You have an argument with him?'

Joe turned away. 'Where's Dick Dean?'

Nobody answered. He walked to the high platform of the Palace. The front door was open, the barroom empty, the dance hall dark. He walked down the street from one keg-and-tincup saloon to another, looking for Dean.

A bartender in a filthy flannel shirt finally said, 'You'll have to satisfy yourself with one notch for tonight, Wolverton, unless you want to pick on some of the local talent, because Dean took it on the high lope.'

*　　　*　　　*

He left Musselshell during the night. At the Lazy M Quarter-circle shack, he slept. It was

250

still raining next day. He was tired, so he took his time and drifted by easy stages toward the home range, stopping one night at Glint Saxon's place on the Little Muddy and spending the next beneath the stars with three cowboys from the TN who were gathering some of Tom Nenus's blooded shorthorns before their stubby legs got run off in the big drag of the Box Elder roundup.

At noon, with the sun shining hot through the washed atmosphere, he rode down on the TN home ranch.

'Joe, I been wanting to see you,' Tom Nenus said, coming out of the house. 'I didn't have a thing to do with that raid on your place.'

'That's water down the crick. I didn't come here on account of that. I wanted to know when the roundup meeting would be.'

'A week from Saturday. You be there?'

'Yeah, I'll be there.' He had an easier way of talking than before. He could see now that Tom Nenus had never meant ill toward him. He swung down and limped stiffness from his legs. 'I'm going to move for redrawing the range lines. When winter comes, there'll be Flying W steers pawing for that long grass down on the Squawhammer, and I want it to be good and legal.'

He ate dinner with Nenus, and riding a borrowed horse, ambled northeastward, avoiding the well traveled trails. It was long after dark when he got to the home corral and started to unsaddle, but a light came on in the house and Ma called his name.

'Joe! Is that you down there?'

He said 'Yes,' and she came to meet him.

It had been a long time since he'd let her take him in her arms. He'd grown so tall he had to bend far over. He was almost six feet, and even with her mothering him he didn't feel like a kid any more.

'Ma,' he said, 'don't cry, Ma.'

'Keep still, you no-good horse wrangler. I'll cry if I want to. What do you mean by staying away so long? Don't you know a body gets worried?'

'There were some men gunning for me.'

'If you mean them two Snaky G curly wolves that were skulking down the creek, you had nothing to worry about. They'll be picking number three buck out of their hindsides from now till Jan'wary. Joe, why'd you leave? If it was on account of—'

'I know all about Holly. I understand how it was. Ellen told me.'

He heard Ellen's voice calling from the house, 'Ma, who is it?'

Ma let him go. She heaved a big sigh and answered, 'Yes, child, it's him.'

He said, 'Is Ellen staying here?'

'She's been here, worrying herself down to a skeleton about you ever since she took her dad out to Miles.'

'The Major didn't—'

'No, he didn't die. They took him to the hospital strapped to a board, but he'll live yet to cheat honest folk. He ordered her back to her schooling at Helena, but she turned around and came here. She says she'll never take another cent from him or set foot in his house again! You try to reason with her, Joe. You tell her she's wrong. That's no way for a child to feel toward her pa.'

She was coming, hastily tying a belt around her ankle-length dress.

'Joe!' she whispered, and it seemed the most natural thing in the world that she should be in his arms.

Grumbling, Ma said as she walked toward the house; 'You're heading for trouble with that Major Eaton. I can feel it in my bones. When he gets out of the hospital, you're headed for trouble.'

But Joe didn't hear her. Nor did the girl whose head was pressed against his breast. Neither of them even realized that she was gone, or that the minutes had passed, until they were startled by a banging on the wagon-tire gong and heard Ma's voice calling, 'Come and get it,' while the savory odor of frying beefsteak drifted past them on the night breeze.

We hope you have enjoyed this Large Print book. Other Chivers Press or Thorndike Press Large Print books are available at your library or directly from the publishers.

For more information about current and forthcoming titles, please call or write, without obligation, to:

Chivers Large Print
published by BBC Audiobooks Ltd
St James House, The Square
Lower Bristol Road
Bath BA2 3BH
UK
email: bbcaudiobooks@bbc.co.uk
www.bbcaudiobooks.co.uk

OR

Thorndike Press
295 Kennedy Memorial Drive
Waterville
Maine 04901
USA
www.gale.com/thorndike
www.gale.com/wheeler

All our Large Print titles are designed for easy reading, and all our books are made to last.